Hitler Never Went to a Hunky Dance

Hitler Never Went to a Hunky Dance

by

D. P. Schnur

PITTSBURGH, PENNSYLVANIA 15222

Dedication

To B. L., my technical support, my confidante,
my sounding board, my love.

D. P.

Author's Note

This is a work of fiction. Those who move through *Hitler Never Went To A Hunky Dance* and its attendant stories are inventions, and any resemblance to actual persons, living or dead, is completely incidental.

Contents

Hitler Never Went To A Hunky Dance...1

A Long Way From The Heart...21

Betcha Can't Catch Me, Margaret..37

Sheep..49

Cows In The Alley...71

Swimming From Washington...81

Major Magnolia...97

The Perfect Silver Bullet...105

Thursday Ablution..117

Prettiest Girl In Cincinnati..125

A Hero's Welcome...135

Coffee Sense...143

Spotty Morgan...149

Hitler Never Went to a Hunky Dance

Henry Uhrmacher was on lend lease from his father, whose store was in Cincinnati, to his uncle, who was not really his uncle, in Louisville. Uncle Fred was a butcher at a chain grocery store that did ten times the volume of his father's small grocery-deli, and he was a life long friend of the family. Fred and his wife, Magdalena, and their two kids had lived in Northern Kentucky until four years earlier, when the grocery chain asked Fred to help establish their first store 'down-river'. Many years prior to joining the chain Fred had worked with Uhrmacher's father, and the friendship had grown deeper and more lasting through the decades, with children from both families refer-ring to the others' adults as 'aunt' and 'uncle'.

In so many ways, Uhrmacher felt that Uncle Fred must certainly be his uncle by kinship. His inherited Uncle understood him, even if he did not always appreciate his actions. Maybe he understood him more than his blood tie family. He was positive that Uncle Fred liked him more than his own father did.

By nature Uhrmacher was inclined more to pensiveness and inactivity than to work, and at age fourteen it had not yet dawned on him that insight would be no more profitable than inactivity. Labor was an unkind intrusion into his studies and thoughts. Financial needs, though they compelled him to work hard in his father's store, had not yet begun to present prolonged difficulties.

He generally kept his mouth shut and worked diligently around his father, out of fear as much as respect. His joking and glib side was reserved for other family members and friends. Uncle Fred tolerated his strange humor and long lapses of introspection more than most. Often, while engaged in a mindless task, he would daydream, and fantasize about his future, or in his Walter Mitty mode, he would engage in flights of fantasy and envision himself in great supporting roles of historical note. If his actions were slowed by such daydreaming, Uncle Fred would simply nudge him back to reality, or offer a loving boot to his rear end to get him to pick up the pace or pay attention to the task at hand. His father, on the other hand, would become angry, and after yelling at him, insist laughingly to anyone willing to listen that Henry was certainly born into the right family. An Uhrmacher, or watchmaker, was perfect, for he seemed to be as cautious with his physical actions as would such an artisan. When alacrity was required, he seemed destined for reverie. Instead of simply emptying the hundred pound sack of potatoes into appropriate bins, or even thrusting handfuls of spuds into the proper receptacles, he was often given to tossing them one at a time. In his mind, it was more important to construct the starting lineup of the 1956 Yankees, or the 1957 Celtics.

He and Uncle Fred had left work early that late summer Saturday and the drive up Bardstown Road had been particularly delightful in the brilliant sunshine. The past few nights had been abnormally cool and refreshing for that time of year, and the accompanying climatic high front produced glorious, warm, comfortable days, which made him think that autumn was ready to make an early appearance. Labor Day was still over a week away, and then he would begin his studies at the prep school where his brothers had gone before him.

He loved riding with Uncle Fred in the faded red Ford pickup. It seemed to suit them both, with its big round fenders, musty, torn seat cover, and radio that only worked sporadically. It rode like a stone, and he loved it. Uncle Fred's cigar even smelled better when they were in the truck. Aunt Mag did not seem to mind his cigars, as long as he did not smoke them in the Dodge, and did not smoke too many in the house, especially at Christmas. And, in her mind they were certainly preferable to his other tobacco habit. He loved to chew Redman, a holdover from his baseball days. Aunt Mag was the most God-fearing, righteous, loveable individual Uhrmacher had ever encountered, and the only time he had heard her utter a foul word was when she described Fred's chewing as the 'shittinest' habit she ever encountered. He only chewed at work and in his own backyard.

The smoke from the corona wafted back into the cab as they turned off Bardstown, then left and right again, onto their street. The huge spreading magnolia that dominated the corner looked so serene and dark green, so pleasant with its spreading shade and waxy curled leaves, that it mad him sad, in a bittersweet way. It was so familiar, and it appeared to be sweating in the afternoon sun. He told Uncle Fred he did not want to go home, and he sure as hell did not want to go to that crummy hunky dance later that evening.

Uncle Fred chuckled and then said, in his W.C. Fields whine, that he was sorry to lose him at the store, and that he really enjoyed having him stay with them the past week. Uhrmacher believed him, and did not want to exit the truck when it was parked in the garage, behind the house, and alongside the big, gray Dodge sedan.

"Y' know, Hank, it was mighty nice of your dad to lend you to me for a week. We needed the help at the store. It's been a chore opening up all the new locations down here, and help's been scarce," he wheezed in that falsely high croak of his. His sentences usually cracked at the end, and trailed off, just like his cigar smoke.

Uhrmacher smiled just listening to him, but he also knew that Uncle Fred was feeding him a line of bullshit so strong it would stun a gorilla. There was no paucity of labor; they were not that busy at the store. He and Uncle Fred would not even be missed on a nor-mally frenetic Saturday afternoon, and his dad had not loaned him out. Uncle Fred had taken him off his father's hands for a week, even when business in the small store in Cincinnati was booming. It was a respite for both him and his father, as close to a vacation as either would ever enjoy. If he drove Uncle Fred crazy, as crazy as he knew he did his father, and he was sure he had caused him some grief over the past week, his surrogate uncle did not register vexation. Instead, he was inclined to lovingly grip him in a loose headlock, or swat him on his butt with one of his ham sized hands, or play catch with him and his son Jeff, after dinner in the backyard.

Uhrmacher repeated that he would give anything to avoid the family style dance in Cincinnati that night.

"Better not let your mom hear you call it a 'hunky dance', Hank, or your Aunt Mag, for that matter," he said, and chuckled in that squeezed, pinched off sound that Uhrmacher found so delightful and comforting. "Besides, we'll all be going together, so it won't be so bad."

"How about Jeff and Evie Marie? They going?"

"No, don't think so," Uncle Fred droned. "At least not Evie Marie. She'll be with Tom the whole weekend, I'm sure. Jeff'll join us, if he gets home from the winery in time. He'll have to get off early, though."

Uncle Fred pronounced his daughter's name in three syllables rather than four, running everything together as 'Evemarie', even though Aunt Mag had always made sure everyone knew her daughter's proper name consisted of two separate two syllable names that held family significance. Evie Marie was a myopic twenty-one year old sec-retary, with long, frizzy blond hair, thick, black rimmed glasses and a body that turned heads when she walked down the avenue. Tom, her fiancé, was a loud-mouthed ex-Marine, who seemed to irritate Uncle Fred with his boisterous overstated nature.

4

Jeff was two years older than Uhrmacher, and drove his twelve-year old jalopy to and from his summer work at a small vineyard and winery in southern Indiana, where he said he was learning the business from the ground up. Uncle Fred snorted when he heard that, and insisted the vintner had better be teaching him something useful, because he was working him to death with slave wages, though he did appreciate the interesting samples his son sometimes brought home.

After showers, and a light snack of fresh boiled ham on dark rye they had just brought home from the super market that day, they were ready to go, when Jeff arrived in a rush. He wanted to go with them to Cincinnati, then balked when he was informed that he would have to stay overnight if he did so. They were to stay at Uhrmacher's parents' house. Jeff had plans for Sunday, and insisted that he absolutely had to return early.

"Well, I'm not gonna drive all the way back here after steering your ma around the dance floor, doing them polkas all night, and drinking beer and eating bratwurst," asserted Uncle Fred. "No sir! Jeff, if you're going, get a move on, but if you do go, you'll stay over with us. We'll head back after mass, and Sunday dinner. It won't be late."

After some insisting, Aunt Mag got all three gentlemen to add ties to their ensembles, and Uncle Fred tossed one of his sport jackets in the back of the Dodge, with Uhrmacher and his son, and they were off on a steady drive up route 42, along the Ohio River. The ride into Cincinnati was pleasant, with the setting sun turning the western sky a burnished old gold, changing later to orange tinted scarlet. As route 42 turned into Dixie Highway in Northern Kentucky, the air felt fresh as it rushed through the open window of the huge sedan.

Jeff inquired where he and Uhrmacher might go, if they found the 'hunky dance' dull and uninteresting. Aunt Mag shot him a look from the front seat that would have killed a lesser man.

"You'll go nowhere in that neighborhood, not at night. It isn't the same as when your father and I went there when we were courting. It was all German and Austrian then. You know, all immigrants. You'll both stay, and dance with young ladies there, or you can go outside with the other boys and joke around, but you'll stay on the grounds of the Germania Hall," she said firmly, then added, "And I don't want any of you calling it that kind of dance again."

She looked at Uncle Fred when she added that last thought. He just chuckled, glanced back at the two grinning teenagers, and tossed his cigar butt out the window.

Uhrmacher's mother said he looked nice when she saw him at the hall, and handed him a sport jacket, a woolen one at that, and insisted he would need it later, when the night grew cooler. His protest gained a postponement. He hung it over the back of his chair at the long table he and his family shared with many other relatives, including Fred and Mag. He said he'd wear it when he inevitably joined the other boys in the front courtyard.

He did not intend to sound insolent, but that is how he obviously appeared to his mother, when he murmured something about not wanting to be at the hunky dance. His older brother was not there, and if it was so important for the entire family to get together in the old neighborhood of her youth, he should have to attend also.

Holding him firmly by the wrist, she jerked him into a far corner of the spacious hall, motioning her husband to join them. Once there, she lectured him in a strained stage whisper. It was a lecture he knew by heart, and he felt awkward and embarrassed by the exercise, because he knew his not-real cousin Jeff was sidling a little closer, to get the whole story. He felt silly because even though he was quite a bit taller than his mother, her presence loomed large as she leaned close to his face and hissed her displeasure. She made him cringe and shrink from her.

Most of the family was there she said, to bid fond farewell to the club. This is the neighborhood where most of them had grown up, and it was a chance to visit with old friends and extended family in a venue that would cease to exist in another year. She lectured about the importance of heritage, and how he should be proud of his Austrian background. As proud of it hopefully, as she and his father were of theirs.

At the mention of the offensive "hunky" term again, she slugged his shoulder, causing him to wince. He caught Jeff, stifling a laugh, out of the corner of his eye.

"Don't call it that," she hissed. "Do you see any Hungarians here?"

"Heck, ma, I don't know. Some of these old Germans are pretty dark and squatty, they could be hunkies," he laughed.

Again, the surprisingly strong right fist thudded into his upper left arm. She was strong for a little wiry woman. She was very angry now, and said using the term was as onerous as referring to colored people as 'niggers', or Italians as 'dagos'.

At the conclusion of her tirade, which was nothing new for him, she recited her litany of favorite Austrian names for which she would be forever proud. Mozart, Haydn, Freud, Mahler, Mendel, all great men, and no one in the family should doubt their importance. Her eyes sparkled, and she seemed to grow another couple inches in stature.

"Wasn't Hitler born in Austria, ma?" He could not resist, even though he knew the jab would earn him another solid punch. He said it as much for Jeff's attention as he did to irritate his mom, and while it resulted in appreciative laughter from his substitute cousin, it also gave rise to attention from his erstwhile quiet father, who rewarded him with a quick whack on the head.

"Shut up now," said his father, quietly but firmly. "You'll enjoy yourself, or else. If you and Jeff want to go outside, go, but eat something first. And, no more talk about leaving and going home, or to the movies, or anything else. Hear?"

Jeff had officially joined their little group by now, and was appropriately somber and chastened, which was not too difficult for him, since his cousin had taken the hits.

"And another thing," his mother divulged in a quietly convincing fashion. "Hitler never went to a hunky dance. I'll bet he didn't dance at all." She was so earnest the two boys had to jump away from getting hit again, they were laughing so hard.

"You just said it, ma," Uhrmacher crowed, as he moved out of his parents' reach. "You'd belt me for using the word."

"That's different. I'm your mother," she said, a little too loudly, as the young men headed for the table loaded with bratwurst, mettwurst, warm potato salad, and sauerkraut.

They hung out with a couple other boys they recognized, one of whom would attend the same all-male prep school in the city with Uhrmacher. They constantly found excuses to leave the hall in between sessions on the dance floor, where they were forced to dance with aunts and female cousins. Uhrmacher was not a bad dancer and did not mind being bounced around the floor a couple times by his wild and drunken Aunt Flo. He could even abide being squeezed between profusely sweating overweight Teutonic couples when he danced with his cousin, Jane, as long as he could escape occasionally to the cool night air.

He spotted her as he and Jeff were reentering the hall after they had transferred his luggage from the Dodge's trunk to the back seat of his father's brand new Ford. She was pale and delicate, of average height, with wheat colored hair. She possessed a slightly aquiline nose, and large, soft, blue eyes. She walked behind two other girls, slowly and gracefully, and smiled shyly at him as they passed each other in the doorway. He caught his breath sharply as she looked straight into his eyes, then pulled her thin, white cotton sweater more closely around her mid-section and continued languidly after her friends. They each turned and looked back at the other at precisely the same instant. Instead of feeling embarrassed or silly, he suddenly felt warm and gooey, and could not wait to shake Jeff. She smiled at him again, not shyly this time, but coyly and with an open invitation in her azure eyes.

As he encouraged Jeff to dance with Jane, he quickly retrieved his woolen jacket from the back of his chair. A quick check of his slicked back dark hair in the men's room mirror, and a few sen-sens popped into his mouth to cover up the knackwurst gave him the courage to look for the pretty blonde with which he was suddenly smitten. A month earlier would have found him cowering behind his short, fat, Aunt Mag in a wild polka, or clowning with one of his buddies, or maybe peeking around a corner, in order to catch a glimpse of the fragile blonde. Now, strangely, he felt a certain urgency to meet and talk with her. Maybe it was his brother's admonitions that he needed to stop dreaming all the time, and stop acting like a 'goon' or 'clown', or he would never cut it in prep school. His brother preached repeatedly that he would need to mingle and socialize with girls from the prep school's sister school, or he would be destined to go through life marked as a misfit. And, while he was prepared to accept the fact that his younger brother would always be considered an oaf, he thought it might be beneficial for him to learn some social graces. Since he started prep school in a matter of days, he convinced himself it was essential to meet her. He did not want to go through life labeled a 'clown'. His brother's admonitions compelled him to track her down.

Perched prettily on the edge of a stone bench in front of the hall, and under the protective branches of a sheltering oak tree, she appeared to be translucent in her paleness. Her pink dress and white sweater contrasted with her red lips, and gave her the aura of a cool, ice cream sundae. A beautiful sundae with a cherry on top, and surrounded by the lovely, light whipped cream of her softly waved blonde hair is how she looked to him. Her pale skin seemed surrealistic in the light of the three-quarter moon and the street lamp, because most kids had sunburned or tanned hides that late in the summer. His own skin shone with a ruddy glow from baseball and grocery deliveries. She obviously avoided getting too much sunlight, or her skin simply did not retain a tint; whatever the cause, it was one more reason why she stood out in his eyes, from all the other lasses at the dance.

Her giggling, plump friends fell silent when he approached, and after he introduced himself, she introduced them to him in almost formal, European fashion. They left after he sat next to her on the bench. Her name was Ingrid, and when she smiled her teeth were dazzlingly white and added to her overall glow, which made his heart race.

"Your friends left," he said needlessly.

"Yes," she said, without making him feel stupid.

"Maybe I should go in and get cokes for all of us." He started to rise, but she placed her hand on his arm to stop him.

"No," she said softly. "They'll be alright. Let's talk, Henry."

No one called him 'Henry' except teachers or relatives, when they were angry with him. It sounded so formal, yet strangely intimate, that it excited him. It felt as though she was staking out a claim on some part of his being, or maybe his past. Maybe it was some act of possession on her part; he did not care, and he did not bother to tell her that all of his friends called him 'Hank'. They talked, hesitantly at first, and he was mesmerized by her lilting voice. Even though they were precisely the same age, down to the month he found out later, he felt immature next to her sophisticated deportment.

They danced the wonderful wiener, or Vienna waltz together, and as soon as it was over, before all the couples that had crowded the dance floor had a chance to scatter, the band broke into a sentimental World War II favorite. He could not remember the name of the song, which was unusual for him, being an avid music aficionado, but he recognized the dreamy melody instantly, and he and Ingrid quite easily and naturally began to glide across the floor to its soft, wonderful arrangement. While the German band did not remind anyone of Guy Lombardo's Royal Canadians, they did not sound like Pete's

Polka Partners either. Even the fat, red-faced tuba player was giving the melody a break, and making ample room for the saxophone and trombone players.

He and Ingrid did not notice that they formed the youngest couple on the floor, and the object of attention of more than a few other approving dancers, including Ingrid's parents. Uhrmacher found it interesting that the band had decided to play a rare sentimental American favorite just when he and Ingrid found themselves in the middle of the dance floor. He could have sworn that the old trombone player had looked soulfully at them when he muted his horn, giving the melody even more depth, warmth, and sweetness. Even Ingrid's height was perfect for him, as a dance partner. She was light and feathery, a wonderful dancer, who responded comfortably to his every movement.

He tried to hold her close, without squeezing her. Breathing in her delicate lavender fragrance, feeling the soft brush of her ivory hair against his cheek, he wondered how he felt and smelled to her. Suddenly, he wished he had splashed on more of Jeff's Old Spice before he left Louisville, and had chewed a handful of sen-sens in the bathroom. Her hand on his shoulder shyly felt its way up to his collar and gently brushed the back of his sunburned neck, causing him to tremble slightly. She instinctively steadied him with her pelvis so they would not lose a step, and all Uhrmacher could do was silently marvel at the moment. Everything had come together so completely, so naturally, so serendipitously, that he was truly astounded. He was not dreaming now, not this time. No imagining playing left field in Yankee Stadium alongside his idol, Mickey Mantle. No mental image of being Bob Cousy's running mate in the back court in Boston Garden, nor of riding alongside Paul Revere to warn the bumpkins of impending danger. No, this girl, this music, this night was real. His brother was dead wrong. He was not a clod. He was not a plodding watchmaker tonight; he was alive, alert, and nimble.

After visiting with their respective beaming families, they rendezvoused at the bench, and began talking intently again, sitting quite close, and gazing into each other's eyes. His cousin Jeff realized they were not going to skip out and goof off at a neighborhood store, and seemed satisfied with dancing, first with Jane, then her stacked older sister. The other guys contented themselves with teasing and laughing with Ingrid's two friends. They were alone on the bench, and alone and engrossed in their thoughts of, and ministrations towards each other.

Unselfconsciously, he removed his jacket and placed it around her shivering shoulders, when he noticed how close to him she was sitting, and that she had fully buttoned her thin sweater.

"Is that okay? I mean, does that feel better?"

"Yes, thank you," she said, demurely. "It feels very warm and comfy."

"It's probably too warm for this time of year," he said, then added, "You know, it's wool, but it's surprising how cool it got tonight."

He looked at the starry night sky, and thought how he had never before noticed how beautiful evening weather could become.

"It feels very soft and warm," she said, continuing to sit close to him. "I hope you don't get cold now."

After admiring the clarity of the sky some more, they realized they were still hungry. Actually, he was not hungry at all, but he offered to get her a sandwich and a coke, and she accepted. He determined that he wanted for nothing except the sound of her voice.

"A bratwurst, please," she chose, "On a rye bun. Not too much mustard."

"Back in a second," he promised.

He looked back, as he entered the hall, and she smiled warmly at him while hugging his jacket.

12

Two bratwursts on rye, one slathered in German hot-sweet, brown mustard, the other with a dab of the pleasingly pungent sauce, and two short, chunky bottles of ice cold coke in hand, and he was on his way back to 'their' stone settee. He had to endure the jokes and jabs of Jeff and one of their buddies, but he was able to dodge any other pitfall and felt fortunate that the kidding was no worse than it was.

He worked his way through the milling throng around the food tables and bar, and was just about to exit the hall when he felt a hand on his shoulder. His Uncle Fred helped guide him outside to the top step of the front entryway. He was just about to fire up a thick cigar when he spotted Uhrmacher trying to negotiate the Teutonic mob.

"Told you that you'd have a good time, didn't I, Hank?" Uncle Fred chuckled, and patted him lightly on the back of his head. He was looking at Ingrid, who was watching them closely from across the small courtyard.

"Yeah, you sure were right, Uncle Fred," he said, looking appreciatively at one of his favorite relatives while enjoying the fragrance of the churchill. "You know, I'm learning a lot tonight. I mean, I'm learning a lot about myself," he hurried to explain.

"Yes, Hank, I'm sure you are," laughed Uncle Fred. "You're beginning four of the most wonderful years of your life. I envy you. Don't waste a minute. Don't miss a moment. Be patient, but soak in every experience you can. Work hard, but enjoy yourself. You're a good kid, Hank, and I know you'll make your family very proud of you."

"Thanks, Uncle Fred. You're a good guy, too," he said, as he noticed his uncle looking again in Ingrid's direction. "She's very nice. I just met her tonight."

"Your Aunt Mag says she knows her parents. Grew up in the same neighborhood with them. Not very far from here, as a matter of fact. She's very pretty, Hank." After hesitating, he gently patted him on the shoulder, and added, "Enjoy yourself, son. Life is too short. I just told Jeff the same thing."

He left Uhrmacher then, to join another uncle on the sidewalk. They smoked their cigars and talked politics, and his nephew immediately missed Uncle Fred's clipped, comical speech patterns. What he had to say always seemed so sincere to Uhrmacher, in spite of his amusing cant.

Ingrid wanted to know with whom he had been talking, and when he told her, he added that his Aunt Mag knew her parents. She told him that her parents knew his folks as well. Wasn't it a small world? Her family still lived in that section of the city, not more than a couple miles from the German hall. Her father knew where his dad's store was, having stopped in previously.

They contentedly munched their sausage sandwiches and discussed many things that each would normally hold so dear and private. They talked of hopes and dreams, plans and fears; things they would not have dared discuss with a sibling, let alone a stranger of the opposite sex. It all felt so right, so natural, that they became oblivious to time and place.

They would be starting high school soon, and while both were products of the Catholic parochial school system, she would be a freshman at a large city school, while he would attend a Catholic boys' prep school. Her father was a laborer at a soap factory, and it was not in the family budget for any of his five children to go to a private school beyond the elementary level. When she told Uhrmacher that she was smack in the middle, with a brother and sister combination that was both older and younger than her, he asked if any of her siblings were also forced to attend the soiree. She said they were all there, and then pointed out a giggling, gangling ash blonde girl, who was busy flirting with a couple of boys, as she dashed in and out of the hall, and around the far corner of the building. He was shocked when Ingrid identified her as her sixteen-year-old sister. She seemed so silly, so immature, so ridiculous, in comparison to the composed, calm, intelligent girl who sat next to him.

14

"You seem older," he said, then hurried to add, "I mean you act like the older sister, not her."

"She has more friends," she said wistfully. "She's very popular. Maybe that's why she laughs so much."

"I think you must be popular, too. You're very interesting," he said. Then he blurted out, "You're pretty, too."

She became unhinged for the first time all night, and blushed prettily. She actually fumbled for something to say, so he saved her.

"I'm surprised you've wanted to spend the whole night with me. I mean, you could have danced with all the other guys, all night long. I'm nothing special."

He was not fishing for compliments. He was being totally honest, and was blunt in expressing his incredulity.

She realized this was the case, and quickly regained her composure.

"I liked the way you looked, and walked. You seemed like such a nice young man, so clean cut. I'm glad you're here."

He was grateful that she called him a young man, and not a boy. It made him feel a little closer in maturity to her.

"I expect you're glad to be going to prep school?" she asked.

"Yes, and you must be glad to be out of grade school also."

"Yes, but I wish I was going to 'Angelus', your sister school. Then we could see each other almost every day, or at least a couple times a week."

"We wouldn't be on the same bus. We'd be on different city buses, on different routes going home, except when I'd be going to work at my dad's store," he said needlessly. He was giving her useless information, but she did not seem to mind.

"I know," she said quietly, and lowered her eyes. "But, we'd see each other once in a while."

"Does it really bother you that you're going to a public school?" He hit the mark, though he tried to miss it.

"Yes," she said, "terribly. The school is so huge, and it'll be full of so many strange kids. My brother and sister have both warned me to be careful who I hang around with."

"You said your grade school started a band a couple years ago. Maybe you could join the band or orchestra in high school. That would be a good group of kids, I think."

"Well, I'd like to," she said. "But, I had to drop out of music classes because I was learning to play the French horn, and when it was time to buy a horn or continue renting one, the money ran out. I'd probably have to start over again in high school, on any instrument they had that they could loan to me, if they'd take a beginner."

Suddenly, she looked sad, and her eyes filled with tears without warning, without fuss.

"Why are you crying?"

"I guess I'm just scared," she said, brushing a tear away. "Aren't you?"

"No. Maybe a little nervous, but in a good, excited way," he said, trying to sound braver than he felt.

"Did your brothers go to the same school?" she asked.

"Yes. It's a family tradition."

"See, you know what to expect. So you don't have to be scared."

"You know what to expect, too," he said. "Your brother and sister have filled you in."

"That's why I'm scared," she laughed, and then added, "You said you loved music, too. Do you play an instrument?"

When informed that he was studying the cornet, she brightened considerably, and seemed enthused that they were both brass lovers. One more thing in common. After a while, she sighed deeply and said again, in a low voice, "I wish I could go to your sister school. I think I'd like 'Angelus'.

He wanted to kiss her, but did not know how. He did not know how to tell her he wanted to kiss her cheek. He studied her face, then slowly moved his hand to her forehead, and gently brushed her softly waved bangs to the side, exposing more pale skin that felt so soft and cool to his touch, he could have sworn it was ivory colored velvet.

She held her breath as she looked at him, and took in every detail of his face. The expression in his eyes made her want to kiss him, but she did not know how. She knew that she would remember this moment, this night, for years to come, and she would be grateful to him for his touch and the expression in his eyes.

"I'm so happy right now, aren't you?" she asked.

"Yes, I am," he said. "I'm happy because you're happy, and because you wanted me to stay with you." He wanted to say more, but felt inadequate and awkward.

"I hope we see each other again."

"We will," he assured her.

"I hope so," she sounded dubious. "But, you'll be with a different bunch of kids. You'll be busy. You won't have time to even call me."

"That's not true!" he protested. "We will see each other. You can always come up to my dad's store on Saturday, when I'm working."

She brightened at that thought, and snuggled close to him.

Their reverie was soon interrupted by his mother's voice, telling him it was time to go, the family was leaving. She was approaching them with a grin on her face, when she noticed he was in shirtsleeves in the chilly night air. She asked him where was his jacket, without noticing it around the pretty, slim, blonde girl, and when he said she had it, his mother smiled indulgently. Before he had a chance to introduce Ingrid to her, his mother was called back to the steps of the hall, where family and friends congregated, hugged, and said good-bye to one another.

"So, it's time for you to leave," she said as she handed him his sport coat.

"Yes."

"Well, you have my phone number. Maybe you could call me sometime. Let me know how school is going, and if you're still playing the cornet."

"Yes, I will." He hesitated. He did not want to leave her, but his father called to him. "I'll want to hear if you got another French horn, or some other instrument. Maybe you'll like it better."

He wanted to clasp her hand, and she wanted to touch his face. Neither did so. Instead, they parted ways, with her walking back to the hall, where the band was playing the last number of the evening, and he hurrying to catch up with his extended family as they walked to their parked cars.

She did not turn round as he looked back from the sidewalk. He caught a glimpse of her back as she entered the foyer of the hall. I hope she gets to join the orchestra, he thought.

Once settled in the back seat of his father's Ford, he felt an odd contentment that mixed with the sweet-sad longing for Ingrid. He wondered if she felt the same way.

The lights of the narrow, old city streets glowed dimly as the small caravan of cars made their way toward Central Parkway. His mother's small head, barely visible over the front seat, turned slightly to the left, as she asked the question he knew she would.

"Well, Hank, did you have a good time?"

"Yeah, ma, I did."

She smiled at his father, and continued, "I knew you would. I knew you'd be happy we made you go."

Time passed, and the streets became wider, the streetlights brighter, and relatives' cars honked softly and quickly, as they turned off at various intersections. Soon, only Uncle Fred's Dodge was in tow, as they got closer to home.

Suddenly, he felt quite sanguine about his coming prep school years. Uncle Fred's advice to be patient, yet enjoy all the coming experiences, still lodged in his mind.

"Ma?"

"Yes?"

"By the time he died and went to hell, I'll bet Hitler never realized what he missed."

A Long Way from
the Heart

The ball came out of the scrum perfectly. The outside halfback scooped it cleanly from the ripped, fragrant turf and lateralled it smoothly back to him, as he veered at half speed to the left and away from the pile of grunting, yelling, cursing men who were fighting for freedom from the jumbled mess of interlocked arms and legs. He moved the smooth, white leather rugby ball to the crook of his left arm as he sped diagonally toward the left sideline from his winger position, and then accelerated to full speed, moving due north on the field toward the opponents' goal line. Keeping a wary eye as defenders attempted to head him off with ruinous tackles, and with no downfield blockers allowed, he knew he was going to get hit hard. He either had to pitch the ball back to a teammate, or attempt a quick drop kick to advance the ball. Knees pumping high, breath coming laboriously, he made his decision and suddenly pirouetted into the air after having run another fifteen yards, and lateralled the ball back toward a trailing mate. He was hit extremely hard by two opponents at precisely the same time. One hit him in his left side, in the space just below his rib cage. He felt the air fly out of his lungs as the force of the blow hit him like a pile driver. It lifted him even higher into the air, and deposited him on his back with such force that he thought surely his spine as well as his ribs had to be broken. The other defender had caught him on his legs, and the strong pressure on his left thigh indicated a sizeable bruise would result. The play continued on, over and past him, as another smallish player from his team took a vicious hit as he advanced the ball with a kick. Their club was small in stature, fleet of foot, and steely in its resolve.

He writhed on the ground as he gasped for breath, instinctively folding his arms across his chest, and then trying to wrap them over his heaving rib cage for support. Though hurt, he collected himself, and bunched his frame into some measure of controlled attack. Both teams set for another scrum, and he joined the fray. Choosing not to limp off the field for the rest of the match, he did not want to cost his team yet another man to injury. People from his sideline were yelling that only two minutes remained until half time. Mercifully, the balance of the half was used up in scrums and mucking about with rucks and little progression of the ball by either side. Nothing close to a try or a goal resulted, and he sank to all fours in the middle of the field as time was called. He felt as if he had been kicked by a Missouri mule, in the ribs, the back, the legs, and in the neck. His white canvas shorts were spotted with blood in several places, and his broad striped red and white rugby shirt wore a mixed pattern of green and brown from the turf, and garnet and maroon from his and other players' blood.

The team had already retreated to its usual halftime resting place under the westward facing steel stands, and by the time he was able to limp over to them they were sucking on fresh oranges and lemons. He grimaced as he gingerly pulled the pulp from the rind of an orange half with his teeth. Even his jaw hurt, though he did not remember taking a whack to his mouth. The coach was looking over his troops, trying to decide who he could not use in the second half. One player who had dragged himself off the field midway through the first half was lost from the game with a severely sprained, hideously swollen ankle. A trainer opined that he might have suffered a break in the bone. Another player was gasping for breath as he clutched his midsection. He had tried to jog a little on the adjoining field behind the stands and could not catch his breath. He insisted it hurt to walk, much less run, and he doubted he could be of any service in the second half.

The coach, a gruff, barrel chested former rugger who still wore his hair in a stiff crewcut almost fifteen years after his college days was not pleased. He cursed and spat as he circled his group of young warriors. They were tied with the visitors, a rough group of oversized kids from a prestigious private college from a neighboring state. They had beaten his team a year earlier, at their place. Now they were here, in his house, and were being given all they could handle, and then some. The blue and gold clad visitors probably had a better team this year; they were certainly bigger and meaner than the previous year, and there were more than the usual couple thousand fans seated in the stands on both sides of the rugby field, as well as straining against the makeshift ropes that held spectators off the playing field. This opponent drew friend and foe alike. The coach insisted he could taste victory and wondered if his charges felt the same way. He screamed and ranted that each man had to dig deeper than they ever did before, that they had to withstand the pain and play if humanly possible.

The team was seriously depleted from two very rough games the previous weekend at a rival state school's field, and the coach and his assistant searched the faces of their tired players for extra determination, deeper persistence.

"What about you, Von Stadt?" The coach stood over him as he sat on the lush, cool grass, eating his second orange half and gingerly probing his side and neck with tentative fingers. "Can you go again this last half?"

The crucible of the classroom having been passed, he faced this test with less certainty. He wanted to jump up and swear his allegiance to the team and the university, and to yell, "Hell yes, coach! Send me in!"

Instead, he glanced up at the scowling, broad-framed figure and said, "Can I, or will I?"

The coach stooped down and fairly spat in his face, "Don't be a smart ass, son. We're down to two extra players, and I need a straight answer."

He glanced away from the coach as he said, "I'm hurting, coach. I think I might have some rib damage, and my leg's killing me, but I'll try it."

The coach gave him a wan smile and tapped him on the sore leg. "That's a long way from your heart, son," he said. "We'll wrap you and the others up. We need everyone out there who's still breathing. We need a lotta heart this second half."

Von Stadt pulled his soaked, heavy cotton uniform shirt up so the assistant trainer could apply oil that felt alternately icy then hot on his skin. Then they wrapped him, too tightly at first, with elastic wrap. The sharp sweet smell of wintergreen and ointment permeated the air under the stands, and several girlfriends of players were drawn closer to the huddle of the young men as they noticed how much adhesive tape and bandage was being applied to bruised and bloodied bodies. The assistant manager quickly wrapped Von Stadt's thigh with tape, and joked how the real pain would come after the match, when the tape was unceremoniously removed, taking leg hair with it.

The coach and his assistant, and the two trainers and equipment manager all left the field a little less than an hour later smiling broadly. They had done their jobs and come away with a tie. They had held the team together with tape, oil, and bandage, the way a World War I mechanic might have kept a Sopwith Camel together with baling wire and glue. The coach insisted the tie was 'like kissing your sister', because no one had won. Yet, the players could tell he was pleased. Against a superior, tough, fast team, they had held together and played over their heads, beyond their immediate capabilities. After giving up a try midway through the second half, they dug even deeper and worked beautiful together. The collisions were vicious, yet they attacked relentlessly, and with screams of encouragement, then of relief from the majority of the crowd, they pushed across with a try as the clock wound down to the closing minute. The conversion was missed, but by then it was just a matter of hanging on for dear life, if not for dear alma mater, to end the match with a tie.

Kurt Von Stadt left the field slowly, savoring the moment. Players from both teams walked off together, along with fans of both schools, congratulating each other on a hard fought game on a gorgeous autumn afternoon. It seemed obvious to him that even though the match ended in a tie score it was viewed as a loss by the visitors, while to the red and white it tasted like victory. As they trudged to the locker room, past the football stadium, past the tennis complex, and beneath the gold, orange, and red leaves of the maples that dotted the sparkling Georgian campus, a friend of his from the opposition gently draped his arm over his shoulders and inquired about his physical standing. They laughed as they compared cuts and contusions, and talked quietly about their plans for the coming evening.

The hot water and foamy suds of the soap in the shower were a welcome reward. The smell of yet more liniment mingled with after shave, deodorant, and cologne and gave off a comforting and almost secretive scent in the locker room; an aroma that made the players feel more like comrades in arms rather than simple rugby players.

He dressed slowly, the softness of his cotton shirt and light cashmere sweater a recompense for the rough treatment his body had endured the previous couple hours. His comfortable slacks felt good against his bruised legs and made him feel less stiff than when he still wore the sweat soaked, filthy, rough uniform.

The sun was flattening in the west and the sky was glowing crimson when he left the locker room, patting the familiar sign affixed to the wall to the immediate right of the door. It read 'Give blood, play rugby'. Each player tapped the message twice during game day, upon entering the locker room prior to the game, and leaving it at the end of the day.

His friend, Tom Herlihy, waited for him on the sidewalk outside the visitors locker room entrance. He was not returning to his campus that evening with most of his teammates. Instead, he was staying over with his friend, Von Stadt, so they could attend a rugby party that evening at an Irish saloon in the Mount Adams section of Cincinnati. Cindy Kolwick, a mutual friend and part-time student at the university, was waiting for them in her car in an adjacent parking lot. She was dressed provocatively in a tight sweater, which did not do much for her tiny breasts, and form fitting slacks which showed off her ample, yet shapely rear end and voluptuous thighs. Cindy lived in a grimy, mid-sized city about ten miles from campus, and she worked as a waitress so she could continue to attend school on a haphazard basis. She was twenty-two and a second semester sophomore, as far as credits earned. Cindy had a heart of gold, very thin straight hair which ended at jaw level, and large bright eyes which were always made up too heavily. Being a rugger groupie, she loved the after-games parties. Thus, she never seemed to mind serving as a driver for guys that did not have cars or rides. She smiled at them both as they climbed in, but saved her intense attention for Tom.

How long had it been? Twenty years. It was a perfect autumn day, just as gorgeous as that Saturday so long ago. Von Stadt walked the beautiful main campus dressed in much the same style as when he left the locker room after that classic match. It was late in the afternoon, and his soft button-down shirt and expensive v-neck wool sweater felt warm and luxurious, as shadows lengthened and the air turned cooler. The years between 1966 and 1986 showed in his face and hairline, but not much in his frame. The few extra pounds he had gained were carried well on his slight build, and he walked the campus purposely, as if he were late for a class, and not just another old grad drifting absent-mindedly across the quad.

Kurt Von Stadt, forty-one years old, slowed his gait as he approached the famous arch in the old biological sciences building. He stopped and looked thoughtfully back at a couple of the historic red brick Georgian structures that crowded the center of the campus, and listened to the campanile peal forth the chimes that sounded the half hour. He turned and continued his stroll through the archway and toward the area of the campus that had once housed the rugby and soccer fields, with their removable stands and bleachers. That area was now a large parking lot and a small block of turf and skinned dirt devoted to softball fields. He had never had a better game than that one. He had never been asked to give anymore of himself in an athletic endeavor than what was requested that day. It formed the apex of his rugby career, when that sport was important, more important than the fledgling hockey team, and before the mandated rise of all the women's sports. Now, if the rugby team still existed on campus, it remained only as a club sport, while the hockey team was important and revenue producing. So many of the old sports were defunct, it was no wonder that side of the campus traditionally given over to athletic arenas, fields and pursuits was changed so dramatically. The balance of that memorable fall, the rest of that glittering season, even through the end of the semester, the ruggers received recognition from many campus acquaintances for that tie against a vaunted foe.

He and Tom Herlihy were friends from their prep school days, with Herlihy going on to the prestigious Catholic university, while he attended the old, academically rich state school. When the two schools played each other, the visitor stayed over and headed back to his respective university the following day. Ruggers were expected to celebrate all wins, losses and ties with equal vigor, and wild parties were the expected norm.

Cindy Kolwick drove rapidly down the state highway toward Cincinnati, glancing furtively at Herlihy seated next to her. Von Stadt sat in the back, and drank in her perfume.

She said, "I think that was the best game I've ever seen. Both you guys played well." When neither young man answered quickly enough, she added, "Are you both beat?"

"Beat, and beat up," said Tom.

"Are you hurt?" She asked Herlihy the question, then glanced back over her shoulder at Von Stadt. Genuine concern toward one, general interest toward the other. She remembered meeting Herlihy two years earlier, when his team had last visited the campus, and she liked him. She had asked Von Stadt to fix them up, but this was as far as he would go in that routine. They were all friends, but he was a closer friend of Herlihy. She agreed to drive, and thus was on her own with regard to her pursuit of his visiting chum.

The saloon was packed with rugby players from several schools, fans, and hangers-on. They located some of their respective team-mates and friends in the back room of the establishment, which was already crowded with players from a nearby university. Those players were still in their dirty, perspiration soaked uniforms, having come straight to the bar from a game on their campus that afternoon. Some still wore their headbands, and most of them were feeling no physical pain from their contest, as the beer and Irish whiskey took hold. One of the local players was a friend of his and Herlihy. He introduced them to his friends and some of the people that had been at his game.

Her name was Gisele Chambrinet, and she was a senior at a local, exclusive women's college. One of her friends dated a rugger at the local school and had talked her into going to the game and the party afterward, as a way to meet 'interesting' men. He laughed when she told him that, and said that ruggers were not interesting, unless you were interested in studying people who had the pathological make-up of serial killers.

"Are you dangerous?" She leaned in close to him so her breast pressed lightly against his arm. Her large, very dark eyes sparkled from excitement and beer.

"No," he said. "I'm not even notorious. I guess I broke the mold for typical ruggers."

She smiled broadly, showing amazingly white, even teeth in a Gene Tierney-like, slight overbite. "What kind of man plays rugby? It's so brutal."

"Cro-Magnon?"

She laughed lightly, easily, exhibiting a bit of pink tongue and throat. Her voice had a soft, lilting quality, with a noticeable French Canadian accent. Her looks were classic Gallic: Black hair worn short, very pale skin, small weak chin, long elegant nose, and a lean, moderately tall frame. She was from Montreal, and had picked the exclusive Catholic women's college because she wanted to attend college in the United States, and friends of her family lived in the area.

By closing time the crowd had thinned noticeably, and the people that were left were hardcore rugby players and fans. The owner of the saloon was a former Irish rugger, and after he had locked up the main bar and turned off the lights, he joined the rest of the group in the dart room in the rear of the establishment. An announcement was made that the saloon was closed, no beer could be purchased, and if anyone wanted to leave they should do so immediately, because the serious party was about to begin.

Two hours later the private party still went on, with singing of bawdy rugby songs, continuous toast of beer and stout among the few members of the three rugby teams still standing, and an impromptu exhibition of female breasts. An amply endowed blonde challenged a rival for her rugger of choice to a face off, or 'front off' as it turned out. When the two girls stood there, topless, facing each other, nipples barely inches apart, the object of their affection did not hoot with glee as did the rest of the party. Wobbling drunkenly, he simply said he thought he needed a comparison with the rest of the women in the room. Instantly, blouses, sweaters, and brassieres were hurled to the floor as most of the women complied. Even Cindy stood there bare breasted, looking ridiculous and sad, with breasts that appeared about right for a slowly developing thirteen year old girl.

Gisele did not partake of the contest, though she laughed and kidded with everyone. She looked at Von Stadt seriously for a moment, then leaned tightly up against him and put her hands on either side of his head, along his ears, and kissed him lightly.

"I'll show you my breasts at the right time," she said quietly. "But not in a room full of people."

He was speechless, and could only nod dumbly. She was the most unique woman he had ever met. He wanted to say something witty, in French, but he could only respond with, "Laissez les bon temps rouller."

She laughed heartily and kissed him again, this time deeply and warmly.

The drive back to campus was long and arduous. Cindy was just as tired as her two companions, but did not have the luxury of being able to fall asleep. She stopped twice on the journey for coffee and doughnuts, and made the two ruggers accompany her into the coffee shops both times. During the second stop, as dawn was breaking in vivid fashion, she told Von Stadt that Gisele had informed her of her attraction to him. She had told her that she thought she loved him, and wanted to "conquer his heart". Again, he was speechless. He had found the young French woman incredibly attractive, intelligent, and exciting, but it had happened too quickly.

"Love doesn't have a timetable, buddy," said Herlihy. "It's pretty obvious to me that she's crazy about you. What's so surprising about that?"

Cindy looked longingly at Herlihy when he said that, but he did not return her gaze.

That was twenty years ago, and it was still too fresh in his mind to not be painful in a bittersweet way.

She stayed in the States after graduation. He graduated within a month of her commencement and took a job with a bank in the same city. The other women in his life, all casual and inconsequential, were soon forgotten. They were consumed with each other, though their love was strained by differences of opinions on everything from politics to the significance of casual sex. They could cross that fine line between love and hate alone on a quiet walk in the woods, or at a social gathering when one viewed the other across a crowded room being eyed approvingly by a member of the opposite sex. She, in particular, felt the need to develop relationships with other suitors when she discerned a desire on his part for a permanent partnership.

By the time he left for his tour of duty in the Army, they had agreed to officially see other people. She felt it honorable to treat their relationship that way, because there was no assurance he would return, and they both had physical and social needs that would have to be addressed. Her pet name for him, 'Mon Cheri', was shortened to 'Cher' as she told him goodbye three days before he left for Fort Dix.

He saw her during a leave after returning to the States, and she was even prettier than he remembered. Extremely pale, even though it was late summer, she had gained a few pounds, and they gave her a softer, more voluptuous appearance. Her hair was still short, just a little longer than in her college days, but still poker straight and glossy black. If corn silk could be burnt and still retain its lustre and strength, he thought it would look like her hair. She was laughing in that familiar open-mouthed fashion, and her shiny hair was tossed back from her cheek as she turned her head to address a question directed at her from another person. Then, she noticed him staring at her.

The party was at a hip little restaurant and tavern on the eastside of town. He was there with a couple friends who worked long and hard to get him to attend the soiree. The restaurant was not far from her old college campus, and he wondered as they traveled to the gathering whether she still lived close by, and if he should try to see her before his leave was up. They had written a total of three letters to each other since he had gone. He had never received a reply to his last one, written over six months earlier. When he spotted her he knew why his friends had invested such effort.

"Hello, Cher," she said softly as she kissed his cheek. "How long will you be home?"

"Not long. I have to leave next Wednesday," he said as he struggled to return her smile.

"You look thin. Are you okay?"

"I'm fine. You're looking better than ever."

"Thanks," she laughed easily now, and continued, "Why didn't you call me when you got in?"

"How come you never wrote to me anymore?" He could not fake a smile anymore, and his heart was aching.

"Ah, Cher. So like you. Answer a question with a question. You know how things are. One gets busy. Careers have to be managed." She waved her hand as if she were mindlessly pushing aside carelessly strung ribbons of gauze. That delicate line was being crossed again.

He told her that he honestly wondered if she could ever make a commitment to anyone, if pride or preoccupation would always interfere. She responded with a shrug, and said she was willing to take the chance that he would not lose interest in her permanently, lack of commitment notwithstanding. They said goodbye when her date caught up with her. Holding her from behind, with both arms around her midsection, the blond young man with startlingly blue eyes was polite to Von Stadt, though it was obvious he was pleased and proud to be the one to squire Gisele that evening. He appeared ready to crow about it. She gently touched Von Stadt's cheek as she excused herself from her date's hold and asked him to wait for her at the entrance to the restaurant.

"Call me when you get back," she said as she left him. Then she turned as she reached the door and mouthed, "Cher".

The years since then flew by. He married a tall German girl after he returned from the service and started a career in a brokerage house in Chicago. He heard from mutual friends that Gisele married some guy from Cleveland that stood to inherit a great deal of money, and then within two years he learned she was divorced and back in Cincinnati.

After his own divorce, two job changes, and three transfers, he found himself working for a financial services company in Michigan. His first Christmas card arrived early that year, just after Thanksgiving, from Tom Herlihy, now a manufacturer's representative in California. His note with the card said that he had recently visited their old hometown and he had seen a number of their mutual friends, including Gisele. She was divorced a second time, had recently returned to the city from Chicago, and was working as a high priced buyer for an exclusive department store. Tom reported she was apparently making a great deal of money, dressed expensively, and at forty one, was better looking than he had ever remembered. In typical Herlihy fashion he wrote that she looked so good, "She made me want to throw rocks at my wife."

Von Stadt laughed to himself as he read his friend's note. They had not seen each other for many years, corresponding only with their Christmas cards. His message elevated his mood momentarily, then brought him crashing down. Tom's closing sentence, that Gisele had asked about him, and that he had provided her with Von Stadt's address, inexplicably depressed him. His insides ached and his throat hurt. He wanted to see her again, but was afraid of the opportunity.

Cards, letters, and a few phone calls ensued in the following months, as Gisele and Von Stadt attempted to reestablish contact, if not a relationship. The last phone call ended in a heated discussion, and Von Stadt could not even remember what precipitated it. It had been late summer and they were discussing the possibility of meeting for a long weekend. She assured him he would be welcome to stay with her, that she would absolutely clear her calendar for him, if he would make the trek back to his hometown. Then the sophomoric argument disappointed both of them, and pride prevented either from firming plans for the appointed autumn weekend. Gisele said she did not think it was wise to always presume they would be between marriages.

Two weeks prior to the designated date he received a terse note from her indicating her anticipation of his visit. She would be waiting for his call when he arrived in town. She looked forward to seeing him, and closed her message by referring to him as "Cher", her favorite rugger.

Kurt Von Stadt continued to walk, slowly now, across the lush outfield grass of the softball field. In the distance the lights of the surrounding dormitories shown mistily as evening settled over the old school. Twenty years. He stopped and crouched so he could pluck a handful of grass and smell it. He could see that young, fleet left wingback slip to the outside and out race everyone for a short while, before being forced to make the graceful, deft lateral. He grimaced as he remembered clearly the tackle that ensued, the searing pain in his ribs and lungs, and the halftime 'call to arms'. He remembered the joy of that day, the high point of the season, of his career. He recalled the comraderie of the teams, the drive to Cincinnati with Herlihy and Cindy, the party at the saloon, the beautiful girl who had kissed him with the most meaningful kiss he had ever experienced in his life. Twenty years and he was here again, reliving and trying to revive a part of his existence that had slipped away. Somewhere, he thought, there was a point where they could have moved in the same circle, but they had not held tightly to each other. They had squandered opportunities, and ignored that most basic of all mandates for lovers: Be gentle with love, because it is so very precious.

Von Stadt stood up and started walking rapidly toward a dormitory on the other side of the field, then stopped. He was talking to himself about his reminiscences, and he shook his head lightly, as if to clear his mind of all thoughts of that day and that night twenty years earlier. Consumed by an odd mixture of guilt and longing, he started back to the parking lot flanking the softball diamond where his car was parked. She was still expecting him. He had not informed her whether he would definitely be there or not, but she insisted she would wait for his call. He stopped a few yards short of the parking area and looked around. This was the spot. He could feel the soft leather of the ball in his hands as he shifted it to his left arm. He could hear the noise and grunts of the scrummage being disengaged, as he cut left and then back again, legs pumping, head swiveling to catch a glimpse of players bearing down on him. He felt the graceful liftoff as he soared into the air, ready to direct the ball to his teammate, ready to feel the imminent collision, ready to experience triumph on the day.

He rapidly walked the length of the parking lot, staying on the thick green grass immediately to the east of it, as these thoughts persistently crowded his mind. He stopped short when he reached the edge of the field where it joined the street. Two girls stood on the sidewalk outside their dormitory, looking at him wonderingly.

He realized he had been muttering to himself again. "I used to play rugby here," he began. "This was a rugby field, a long time ago. I played on the team."

The girls did not acknowledge him, and he turned away quickly in embarrassment, and started walking toward the parking lot and his car.

Betcha Can't Catch Me, Margaret

She was twelve years old during the summer of 1923, and that seemed to be a terrific year to her, full of promise and fun. Hard work mixed with adventure, and interesting encounters with family and strangers occurred on a regular basis. The spring of that year brought tales of wonderment from far away cities like New York and London and Paris. She heard one of her brothers telling their father of the presentation of a motion picture with sound. Sound-on-film was how he referred to it. The title was "Phonofilm", and the thought captivated her. Her other brother showed her a picture of a "castle" in New York. Actually, it was a ballpark, which had recently opened and it was called Yankee Stadium. He read its description from the newspaper, and while she cared not a whit about baseball, she knew the name of its star tenant, Babe Ruth, and was transported magically in her thoughts to that wonderful city and its magnificent edifices.

Closer to home she was witnessing the draining of the Miami-Erie Canal, that tawdry, squalid body of water which had served the city in which she lived for almost one hundred years, but was long obsolete and not worthy of much trade for the past two decades. Still, it was exciting for her and her sisters to venture to the various job sites to witness the building of a new subway, directly under the old canal. Along with hearing about subway lines elsewhere in the world, it allowed her to dream of faraway places and exciting people.

The old canal marked the southernmost portion of her neighborhood in the Over-The-Rhine section of the city. Populated almost exclusively by Germans, Austrians, and a few Hungarians, it felt foreign to most visitors, and even to some natives from other sections of the city. The atmosphere was strictly Teutonic. The music, the food, the beer, though illegal, was German. Most of the conversation in the streets, the small shops, if not the large stores, and certainly in the homes and apartments was German. And, while German had not been taught or utilized as an implement for instruction in elementary schools since the end of the Great War, the language was still interspersed on a regular basis with English in the conversations in school rooms and playgrounds.

She and her sisters spoke English to each other, and to their cousins who lived next door. To their parents, they spoke a mixture of German and English. Their cousins, Joe, Frank, and Motz, followed the same communication formula in their family. The boys' mother, Margaret, seemed to appreciate, if not actually enjoy the healthy mix of the two languages.

Margaret was the young girl's mother's sister-in-law, and was very proud of her Austrian lineage. Her mother and her uncle, Margaret's husband, downplayed their heritage, however. Supposedly, they came from a town in Europe not more than thirty miles from where Margaret grew up, but Margaret looked "more Austrian" in the girls' eyes. She was taller than her sister-in-law, though at five feet two inches, that hardly made her statuesque. She was also rather fair skinned, with light brown hair and hazel eyes. The girl's mother and her uncle had a slightly darker look, with very dark brown hair, and short, almost squat frames. Aunt Margaret wondered, often aloud, if there was not some Hungarian blood in their family. She questioned whether the Hungarian side of the Austro-Hungarian empire had not crept into their family, therefore making them appreciate things

Hungarian more than was otherwise fitting. Whenever one of her sons talked about what the teachers in school said about all the kids in the German neighborhood, Aunt Margaret was quick to point out that they were Austrian. They might speak German she insisted, and share many of the same experiences as their neighbors, but they had come from Austria, not Germany. The supposed superiority of the position was lost on her children, and their cousins next door.

The young girl was the first offspring in her family born in America. Her older siblings had been brought to this country by her parents, at precisely the same time as her aunt and uncle next door and her cousin Joe. Only Frank and Motz were Aunt Margaret's new-world products. While Josef was "Joe", and Franz was "Frank", only the youngest cousin, Mathias, was referred to in the vernacular "Motz". It may have been Aunt Margaret's method for claiming her youngest for the old country. A small token or tie, as it were to the fatherland. She loved it when Aunt Margaret and her mother described towns and settings they had experienced in Europe. Aunt Margaret had spent a few weeks in Vienna as a child, visiting relatives, and she was forced to repeat descriptions of that visit over and over again to her young niece. She never got tired of hearing about the shops, the music, the clothes of the day. Even the little cakes, torts, and treats that were enjoyed every afternoon between four and five o'clock, at der kaffee und kuchen, were a direct link to the old country. That was a custom to which Aunt Margaret and the girl's mother clung fiercely. Since dinner in both households was not until seven or later, a little sweet snack late in the afternoon satisfied both sisters-in-law, and their active children.

The young girl insisted Aunt Margaret go into great detail each time she waxed poetic about life in the old country. Her mother, on the other hand, dismissed such talk as drivel, and reminded them all that if life in Europe had been that rosy, they would not have immigrated to the United States. Furthermore, even though life was tough here, and everyone had to work long, hard hours, they had jobs. Here they had an income, and they probably would not have any security back in Austria, or Germany, or Hungary, or anywhere else in Europe right now.

Aunt Margaret would smooth her niece's auburn hair, and switching back to her halting, faulty English, insist soothingly that Europe was still beautiful, even though it was going through rough times after the war. She emphasized that it was still a civilized part of the world, despite what her mother thought and said. Also, even though many people had always lived in close proximity to each other, they did not have to live like this; and she would spread her arms expansively, and gesture as though she were indicating the entire North American continent. Instead, she was referring to the Over-The-Rhine neighborhood where they lived now, with narrow shotgun houses separated only by walkways, with some flimsy wooden fences separating tiny backyard patches of brown grass. If a neighbor really wanted to demonstrate some conspicuous wealth, they tore down the frame fences, and walled off their patch of dirt with brick. Most families did not have those kinds of resources, and if they did, the money was spent on items inside the house.

She did not think they were poor. No more so than any of the other families that lived in the Mohawk portion of Over-The-Rhine, which got its name because it attracted so many German immigrants to that section of the city. The old doomed canal was as close as they could come to a replica of the Rhine River. The Ohio River, loaded with steamboats, barges, and other vessels of commerce, and lined with "cut and shoot" saloons, and houses of ill repute, would certainly not suffice. When Aunt Margaret talked wistfully of times and places long ago, and sometimes crooned old, half forgotten love songs, the young girl was transported out of the neighborhood, and aunt and niece appeared joined in some wonderful, mystical fashion that their relatives did not understand. Her mother and sisters would observe this behavior and shake their heads and joke among themselves. Both of them seemed to be useless dreamers at those times, and there was so much work to be done. When Aunt Margaret sensed they were being critically observed, she bounced from her chair, knocking the young girl over, who had been resting her head on her aunt's knee. Or, she'd bolt upright, and gently swat her niece on the butt, as she jerked her to her feet. Always in English then, she would chastise her, for luring her into dreamland, into wasted moments that made it difficult to return to "this", and she would gesture wildly about herself again.

The young girl knew better. Aunt Margaret liked dreaming as much as she did. She liked hearing stories about faraway places, about people who led magical lives, about adventures that might seem ordinary to special people, but were special to them, and Aunt Margaret loved telling them. When Aunt Margaret held her chin in her curiously smooth hand, she felt somehow secure. Her mother's hands were rough, but Aunt Margaret's always felt smooth, though she worked just as hard as her mother, performing the same tasks on a daily basis. She knew that Aunt Margaret meant no harm, indeed, she was probably giving her a compliment when she said she was a dreamer, or that she would amount to nothing if she did not stop dreaming so much. She offered these criticisms in a soft manner, always stroking the child's head or her cheek, or cupping her chin in her hand. She insisted that her niece was not as pretty as her sisters, especially her older sister Mary, who was petite, pert, and fifteen. When she saw that she had deflated the child, she quietly reminded her that many disappointments awaited her in life, and that she could not dream them all away.

She always felt better about herself after spending time with Aunt Margaret, even if such times proved to be an emotional roller coaster, because she knew that she and her aunt connected in a singular way that a woman with no female children could with a female child who did not feel appreciated by her own mother. Aunt Margaret would often dismiss her with "schlafen madchen", dreamer, or butterfly, and send her home or on an errand.

The Notre Dame sisters, the nuns who instructed the local kids who went to the elementary Catholic School were not as tolerant. Strict disciplinarians, they found very little in the neighborhood to be of redeeming social value, and saw precious little humor in the world. She was not a good student, and was constantly accused of being a dreamer and there was nothing remotely complimentary about that label when applied by them. When she was teased by her cousins or her younger sister about being ridiculed by the nuns, she sought consolation from her aunt, who recognized that this particular child would always have a wistfulness intertwined with necessary industriousness.

On the last day of school in early June Sister Antoinette chided her for being late for morning formation. The nun derided her for never paying attention, for not listening to directions or warning bells, even on the last day of classes. Little did the nun know that it would indeed be her last day in that particular school. She was told that evening by her parents that she would follow the path of her older sister, Mary, and complete two more years of school, in a public vocational institution, before entering the work world. Mary had a job at Alms and Doepke, a large department store just a short streetcar ride away from Mohawk, and she had landed the position straight out of school. She worked as a sales girl in the millinery department, and loved it. Her sister felt even giddier that summer knowing she would never have to return to the nuns, and their constant brand of humiliation. Aunt Margaret knew how she felt and told her the biggest crime the nuns were guilty of was knocking the dreams out of kids.

Aunt Margaret was slow to anger, but the one thing that caused her to lose her temper fastest was disrespect from children. She had three wild boys to constantly corral, and they proved to be especially exasperating. Joe, the oldest, persisted in tormenting his younger brother, Frank, with the most ridiculous, insignificant slights and gestures imaginable. It only worked with Frank because he had such a violent temper, and was jealous of everything and anything Joe had or said. He craved attention as the middle brother, and went into a rage when he saw Joe getting more than his fair share. Joe was a class clown and could drive his parents, and most other adults crazy with his antics. The more people exhibited irritation, the more animated he became. Motz, the youngest, cried a lot, and laughed only when he saw his brothers in trouble. He brought up the rear end of the action in any games played by the neighborhood boys in the narrow streets and alleys. The boys were six years different in age, three years between each one. The girls loved living next to their cousins. They loved their clowning and kidding, their fighting and yelling, their proximity during good times and bad. She often felt sorry for Aunt

Margaret, trying to raise three wild kids, then she would realize her aunt tolerated much in each of them that made them so incorrigible.

During a heated argument between her sisters one day when their mother was out, Aunt Margaret yelled at them from an open window that looked directly into their kitchen, across the narrow walkway separating the two houses. Mary was late for work, and was laying down the law and issuing orders for the day, or at least until their mother returned. Her younger sister obstinately told Mary she did not have to obey her, and she would do as she pleased until their mom resumed control. The young girl was pleading with them both to shut up, as the entire block could probably hear the argument when Aunt Margaret interjected, and was told promptly by Mary to keep her nose out of it and pay attention to her own kids. "Old Cow!" shouted Mary, as she slammed the window shut and left for her job.

Aunt Margaret was over in a flash, berating the two younger girls for arguing and for insulting her, even though she knew Mary was the main culprit. That evening, after both families had finished supper, Aunt Margaret was going over the same subject in their kitchen with their mother. She was exercised about the experience largely because of Mary's lack of remorse. If that was what working in a department store was doing to her, better she went back to the nuns for more discipline! Their mother patiently explained that Mary was simply taking her place that morning, and certainly meant no disrespect. Later that night she forced her oldest daughter to go next door and apologize to her aunt.

Aunt Margaret felt minutely better after Mary talked with her even though she realized the girl was forced to apologize and doubted the sincerity of the contrition. She may have become quickly angered when children drove her to distraction, but her civility allowed her to compose herself swiftly, even if she suspected the motives and words behind subsequent apologies were tainted.

Joe was particularly adroit at getting his mother's goat. He loved to goof off when he was supposed to be doing chores, until she could not take it anymore and went after him with a large wooden spoon.

The harder she whacked him on the rump with the spoon the more he laughed and joked. Then he would start running through the house calling her nonsensical names and she would chase him with the spoon, alternately laughing at him and crying hysterically. When he became insulting, she actually tried to hurt him and started swinging wildly at his back and shoulders. She would get close enough to really haul off and belt him when he would dance away, sometimes with backward steps, all the while laughing wildly and mimicking her. Down the steps they would go to the first floor and into the spacious kitchen with the large square table in the middle of the room. There he would completely torment her, waving his arms and spitting at her. Sobbing and screaming at him, she would attempt to spit back as he kept the table between them. The other two boys would join in the fray then, with Frank screaming at Joe to leave their mother alone, and Motz rooting his mother on, with "pound him, ma!"

Joe would hesitate slightly as his mother rounded a corner of the table and got close to clobbering him with the spoon, then dance away from her again and taunt her with, "Betcha can't catch me, Margaret!"

Aunt Margaret was furious and screamed in German, "I'm your mother! You show me some respect, you hoodlum!"

The game would go on until he ran outside and up the walkway to the street. Exhausted, Aunt Margaret would slump onto a kitchen chair, and be comforted by Motz, while Frank swore to his mother that he would kill his brother when he came home.

This scene or one similar to it, was played out at least once a week, and sometimes the chase took place out into the postage stamp- size backyard, or in the walkway between the houses, or in the street in front of the residence. The girls next door were amused and horrified. They laughed with the boys and cried with their aunt. They alternately enjoyed and detested all of the commotion, but they loved living next door to their wild cousins.

Once, Frank grabbed a butcher knife and chased Joe into the backyard, threatening to kill him because of a perceived slight. Joe laughed and dodged to and fro, avoiding Frank's clumsy lunges. Motz had been throwing buckets of water over the fence at two of his cousins, and they were squirting him with a garden hose. It was a refreshing exercise on a hot summer afternoon, but their squeals of delight turned into screams of horror when they saw the gleaming instrument slash toward Joe. He had no intention of allowing Frank to get too close to him, and tossed large clay flower pots and wooden milk bottle cases in his path until he could escape through the walkway to the street. Frank was in hot pursuit, the girls and Motz close behind and laughing heartily again now that a homicide was not imminent, until Aunt Margaret stopped them all in their tracks with a stern warning.

When asked why he had chased his brother with the knife, Frank responded by telling his mother that Joe had referred to a friend of his from two streets away as a "hunky", and when he protested, his brother told him he looked like a "hunky" too. Aunt Margaret understood why her volatile son had gone temporarily insane, and assured him that Joe "would get it" when he returned home. Being called "hunky" was about as vile an insult as could be hurled at a German or Austrian kid in that neighborhood. The term, an epithet for Hungarian, was tossed at any kid that looked a little too dark or swarthy, or was built a little too wide and close to the ground, or whose last name did not sound "right" for the neighborhood. A child could be named Santelli or Aiello, and they would be labeled "hunky". It was a fighting word indeed, and Aunt Margaret recognized it as such. She assured Frank that his brother would stop calling him that name, if he just did not get so upset. She knew the advice was futile; if she were Frank she would be as equally upset. Frank's attempts to "kill" became legendary, and eventually routine. For a while it became a weekly occurrence: Joe laughing, dashing about, and calling Frank "hunky", Frank, knife in hand, oozing hatred and literally frothing at the corners of his mouth, chasing him into the backyard and sometimes into the girls' yard, and Motz bringing up the rear, yelling he was going to tell ma. His mother could have been a deaf mute, one hundred miles down river in Louisville, and she would have known what was happening. Everyone within four blocks knew that Frank was killing Joe again.

One early evening, just as their father was coming home from work at the factory, the boys had a row and Frank grabbed the knife. The girls watched with amusement as the back door of their cousins' house flew open, and out came Joe, hopping as he ran, trying to get his shoes on and stay safely out of harm's way.

"Ooh, ooh, ooh," hissed Frank, spittle being tossed from his lips as he seethed with anger. "Don't you ever call me a hunky again, you, you!" He stammered and swung the knife toward his brother in an awkward fashion. Finally, he stopped short, and breathing heavily, screamed the only insult his feverish brain could work up at the moment. "You're a hunky! You're the hunky in our family!"

His triumphant look and feeling of exultation was short lived, as Joe laughed even harder. "If I'm a hunky, that makes you the brother of one, so you're a hunky, too!"

The girls laughed mightily at that, which threw Frank into an even greater rage. This time he might really have killed Joe, if he had caught him, but Aunt Margaret calmly put an end to the evening's entertainment when she announced that supper was ready. Frank told her he was not coming in until he had killed his brother, to which she responded, "You can kill him tomorrow, now come in and eat."

When told they were having potato soup with dumplings and eggs, Frank willingly surrendered the knife and started discussing baseball scores with his brother, Joe, as they entered their house.

The young girl often discussed hurt feelings and insults with her Aunt Margaret. She did not understand why people insulted one another, and even though she knew her cousins did not really hate each other, it seemed to her that they would have to remember many of these slights as they got older. Some of these hard feelings would have to remain with them for a long time. She would never forget some of the things that were said to her by the nuns. She told her Aunt Margaret that some of the things Joe said were more than just unkind, they were downright cruel.

Aunt Margaret would look long and lovingly at the ungainly child. She wanted to tell her not to be so sensitive, that it would harm her more than she knew if she took everything to heart, if she remembered too much. But, she did not, could not tell her this. She saw the sensitivity, yet the absolute ability to forgive in the child, and knew that telling her not to be that way was futile. It would be as impossible for the child to slough off certain things, as it was for herself. Instead, she would explain carefully, over and over, to try to recognize people's limitations, and forgive them even if you could not forget words and actions. She also reminded her niece that, as Austrians, they had music, art, culture and joy in their heritage, and not to let someone else's words or deeds diminish that fact.

Late that summer, Aunt Margaret had been involved in a particularly violent argument with Joe right at suppertime. When her husband arrived home, he took Joe's part, after cuffing him about the ear and sending him inside. Her husband had called her foolish, and said she appeared as childish as the boys did when she engaged in such behavior. All this took place loudly in their backyard, and everyone on either side of their house heard it all.

Long after supper was over, and most neighbors had retreated from their front porches, back into their steamy shotgun houses and bungalows on that hot, humid night, Aunt Margaret sat on her porch swing. Everything was silent when the young girl went next door to sit with her aunt. After crooning to her, and smoothing her soft hair, Aunt Margaret went inside to get some lemonade. As they creaked back and forth on the swing, drinking the lemonade from sweating dark red glass tumblers, the niece noticed her Aunt's red, swollen eyes. She empathized with Aunt Margaret, and offered the opinion that her uncle had been wrong, and he should not have said such harsh things to her.

Her aunt looked at her carefully and asked in English, "You heard everything?"

"Yes," said the child with wide-eyed honesty, "We all did."

Her aunt barely stifled a deep, shivering sob. The child knew that her aunt now felt worse because of her revelation and assured her that it was okay. Everyone in their house was on her side. She told her aunt that she loved her, and was sure her uncle loved her also.

"Yes," said Aunt Margaret. "I know he does. So do the boys. Sometimes people just can't help from hurting other people. Sometimes they hurt people they love because they don't know how to say they love them."

Her niece considered this as she set her glass down and laid her head in her aunt's lap. Instinctively, Aunt Margaret began smoothing her hair again and whispering little loving words to her. When she asked her aunt if she really loved her also, Aunt Margaret smiled down at her and said, "Ah, liebchen, maybe I love you best."

"Even when you say I'm not very pretty, or I shouldn't dream so much?"

"Yes, liebchen. Then, most of all."

Sheep

The bar was packed and all the bartenders were rushed. Nonetheless, when Sal saw him at the end of the bar he immediately drew a cold one from the Bud tap, and personally walked it down to him, carefully dodging other yelling, swearing, sweating bartenders who protested he was deserting his post. Len Reinhardt asked Sal why there was such a big crowd on an early spring Tuesday night.

"Oh, Uncle Ralphie's doing his thing in the back room. He's in for some promotion. Not sure who's sponsoring him," said Sal, looking disgusted. Sal's black eyebrows nearly met over his nose, and when he frowned they practically knit into a thick fuzzy rope from one temple to the other.

He continued, "I gotta get back to my station, but hang around, I'm done in an hour and we can have pizza, and talk." He pointed at the beer he had served. "This one's on the house, but you're on your own 'til I'm off."

The erstwhile bartender scurried off, and the recipient of his largesse spoke with a couple harried waitresses that he knew. They were all students at the local state university, an institution noted for its academic excellence, stunningly beautiful campus, fine athletic teams, and lively watering holes.

Uncle Ralphie, a quasi-celebrity from a television station some thirty-five miles away was in town for a combined fraternity-sorority blow out. It was not Reinhardt's fraternity, and he found it interesting that the house that was sponsoring the event had the kind of clout that could get Uncle Ralphie into town during the middle of the week. It was also noteworthy that the event had outgrown the fraternity house and had to be moved to one of the larger uptown bars. The evening was designed to build interest for the coming annual Greek week. Uncle Ralphie was famous for attending all types of campus activities. He also served as spokesman for a local brewery, which encouraged his involvement in campus parades, celebrations, homecomings, and hi-jinks. Uncle Ralphie also liked drinking beer and fondling college co-eds.

Later that evening, when his shift was over, Sal sat in a rear booth with his fraternity brother and confidante, eating leftover unsold pizza and drinking cold beer. The crowd had thinned noticeably.

Reinhardt asked Sal if the free beer was Bud or Schlitz. It was rather, the brand that sponsored Uncle Ralphie. "We got extra barrels in because of his appearance," said Sal. "But we didn't sell nearly enough. Hell, we were giving it away the last half-hour he was here." They drank and ate and began musing about what might happen the following day on the college baseball field.

"This is it for me, buddy," said Sal. "I don't make the team this year, I'm done. I know I can play, I know I can hit. I just want the assholes to take a good look. Not like last year. What was it? Three or four swings in the cage, a couple ground balls hit to me, and that's it! No thanks, we don't need you! Geez, I know I can play. I was damn good in high school."

They were juniors, and this would be Sal's third try at making the team. He was easily and quickly dismissed as a freshman, but after a great summer of recreational ball back in his native Syracuse, he thought he had a legitimate chance the next year. The result was the same, another rapid rejection. He had an even better year at class A amateur ball in upstate New York last summer, and was eager to give the college game one more try. While making the team did not guarantee a scholarship, he knew that this would be his last attempt. There were few baseball scholarships given at the school. The players on full or partials, and a few walk-on holdovers from the previous year who hoped to get some monetary help made up the core of the team. A couple senior football players who wanted to play baseball and had no more spring football practices to worry about augmented the roster. The team had been working out in a campus gymnasium for the past week and a half, and was ready to move outside for the season's first real drills. For the next three days the team would be practicing at their home field on the eastside of their campus, behind the historic football stadium. During those three days the coaching staff, a cranky, bandy-legged head coach, and Buddy Collins, the nice guy part-time coach, would also look at a number of walk-ons, and pick a few of them to flesh out the squad. By the middle of the following week the team would be headed south, to play itself into shape and work its way back north.

Sal told him the team was not going to Florida this year. They were going to Savannah to play in a tournament, then start playing individual games as they moved north and west through Georgia. Sherman's march in reverse! He said they were going to play some top notch teams down there: Clemson, Georgia Tech, Tennessee, Georgia, and a couple others. Sal was a font of knowledge and possessed a tremendous intelligence system, since he had dated most of the girls in the athletic office as well as those in administration. If something needed to be researched, Sal was the man. A very handsome guy, he had hairy arms and legs, and a massive hairy chest to go with his broad, strong stature. He needed to shave twice a day if he had a date in the evening, and his wiry black hair was thinning at the crown. Large dark eyes flashing and glistening, he told stories and jokes, laughed heartily with his friends, and easily charmed women. A sharp dresser, he talked rapidly, and used his hands expressively. He could always fix a friend up with a nice looking date at the last minute. Women loved him.

Reinhardt went out for the team for the first time the year before because Sal talked him into making the effort. Sal could talk most people into almost anything most of the time. Reinhardt had not played baseball since prep school, but at Sal's insistence he went with him to the open practice. As an average player, though very fast, he did not care if he made the team or not. It just was not an important activity for him. Not so with Sal, who knew he could play and just wanted the chance to prove it. Sal talked and enthused about their chances, and the fire built in the other potential substitute, as they started on another pitcher of beer. Just making the team meant possibly seeing action when the regulars were back from the Savannah trip in less than three weeks.

Asked how many extra players would be chosen, Sal considered at length and replied, "Based on who they got coming back, and knowing they'll make room for Markey, I think they'll take three, maybe four. As far as how many will be there tomorrow, it'll depend on the weather. If it's okay, there'll probably be a lot."

Bruce Markey was the former quarterback whose eligibility in football was done, so he decided to give baseball a try. Word was he could throw aspirin tablets through a barn wall, so they would probably give him a spot. He would not cost them a scholarship either.

"'Woodenhead' needs help this year," said Sal. "He lost a lot from last year's team. And, that kid from Florida, that speed burner in the outfield got homesick. He's transferring to Florida State. At least that's what Joanie told me."

Joanie was Sal's primary source of information in the athletic office, and 'Woodenhead' was his irreverent nickname for Coach Woodscrim, the pugnacious, hawk-faced, little baseball coach.

Sal was uncharacteristically pensive when he said in a low voice, "I know I can hit, if they'll just give me a good look." Then he brightened and added, "They need outfield help. Hell, I'm strictly an infielder, I can't play the outfield and no way can I run with you. With your speed, I like your chances."

Reinhardt responded, "I don't care if I make the team or not. Rugby is my sport, it's what I enjoy. I'm only going to support you in your efforts."

Sal snorted, "Yeah, don't do me any favors. You want to make it too. Maybe not as bad as me, but you wouldn't be doing it again this year if you didn't want to wear that uniform. The difference is, you like baseball, and I love it."

Sal had a classic big hitter's frame, while his friend was slight and built sparingly. Though they were about the same height, Sal out-weighed his good friend by some thirty pounds. Reinhardt knew that his size, as well as his lack of passion for the game, would hinder his chances.

The day was overcast yet warm for the beginning of March. The temperature was in the 60's, and the air was humid. Rain or some-thing hung in the air. His drab, gray, well worn visitor's uniform was at least two sizes too large, and draped him like a cheap suit. The red script on the front of the shirt, as well as the red numbers on the back, and the red sleeves of the underjersey were faded to a deep pink. The scarlet red cap and bright red stirrup socks, however, were brilliant in their newness.

As they took their place with the other hopefuls in the stands down the third base line, he noticed how green the outfield grass looked. It seemed artificial, since it had been abnormally warm for several weeks, and spring was making an early appearance in southern Ohio. There were not as many players trying out as he would have guessed. Maybe fifteen gray clad young warriors sat in the stands lis-tening to Coach Woodscrim telling them how fair the tryouts would be, and how each player would be given an honest chance to make the team.

While the coach talked, Reinhardt surveyed the classic beauty of the old baseball field. It looked pristine in its purity. The symmetrical nature of the chain link outfield fence topped by a thick, dark green rolled top cover framed the entire setting. The freshly cut outfield and infield grass, so green so early, made the soil of the basepaths look that much darker. The entire field seemed to be manicured. Battleship gray steel stands down both baselines were empty, save for the walkons, and gave off a feeling of stability, of permanence. Directly behind home plate low stands were topped by a compact press box, and provided an excellent view of the scoreboard beyond the right center field fence.

The scholarship players and those who had already made the team were dressed in new, creamy white uniforms, and were running wind sprints in the outfield. Their uniforms, with fresh scarlet script spelling out the university name, and matching red numbers and stirrup socks, looked beautiful against the emerald green outfield grass. As they ended their particular sprints, the players flounced and bounced on the spongy turf.

"Sheep," Reinhardt whispered to Sal, motioning to the white clad players.

"What?" Sal looked bewildered and slightly annoyed. He was drinking in every one of 'Woodenhead''s words.

"They look like sheep. The regular team. Look how white they look in the outfield. They look like sheep, some of them running and some just grazing."

"Yeah, well I wouldn't mind getting a white suit by Friday. You can call me a sheep, if I make the team."

Coach Woodscrim ended his sermon by glaring at the two of them, and then sending all of the hopefuls over to his assistant, Buddy Collins, for calisthenics and the first few drills of the day, with a snarled, "Let's go, girls!"

Buddy Collins was a nice guy, a holler guy, a not-too-bright individual who was in his fourth year of a two-year Masters program in physical education. Baseball was not his primary sport, but it had been assigned to him for three years running, and he enjoyed the players and trips down south. Sal's theory was that Buddy would escape Woodenhead as soon as he had completed his graduate study and could get an assistant's position on the football team. Sal also wondered how much intelligence it took to be able to instruct someone in the fine art of holding a tennis racquet by its handle. "Isn't that what he's studying?" was Sal's take on the subject.

That evening in the fraternity house, after dinner and a couple hours of intense study in the library, the two friends sat in the upstairs television room discussing that day's practice, and the fact that they were still alive in the eyes of the coaches. Six "wannabees" were still in the hunt, and they were two of them. Sal was elated, as much as anything by the fact that it had vindicated him for quitting his part-time job at the bar.

In order to enjoy rugby and a work free autumn, Reinhardt had to work hard in spring and summer. His enthusiasm for the baseball team waxed and waned in consort with Sal's emotions, but he felt guilty about suspending his own part-time job working in one of the women's dining halls just because of baseball.

Bantering with his fraternity brothers, Sal insisted, "It's the Yankees or nothing for me. Born a Yankees fan, I'll die one too. I see myself playing along side Tresh or Richardson."

A commotion on the fire escape in the back of the house interrupted everyone. The wind and rain, which started several hours earlier, were intensifying. They opened the window to find a fraternity brother in an inebriated state, clinging with one hand to the rail of the dilapidated fire escape. It shuddered ominously under his weight, but he clutched a half empty bottle of Black and White scotch in his free hand.

"For chrissake, what's Timmy doing?" shouted one brother.

"At least he's drinking something good," laughed another.

"How the hell did he get out there?" yelled still another. "Christ, he must have climbed from the backyard. That goddamn thing isn't safe, it's rusted and loose."

"Well, he's out there now," said Sal. "Let's get him in here before it collapses."

A couple brothers cautiously stepped on to the platform, and it made a terrible groaning, cracking noise. Tim was laughing wildly as they jumped back inside, and the frame began to sag in serious fashion. As he continued to swig from the bottle he started rocking, and the contraption eventually broke away from the back of the building. One side of the frame held fast, but the ladder was dislodged, and the entire thing listed precipitously. He was enjoying himself as he swung back and forth, moving toward and then away from the house at a slanted angle, as his fraternity brothers were becoming ever more nervously raucous.

During one of his trips toward the house, two of his mates secured the swinging pendulum long enough for the two ballplayers to reach him and pull him to the open window. Working as a tandem from adjacent upstairs windows, several young men were able to keep the frame steady long enough to get their wayward brother into the room. He flopped on the floor like a wet seal and promptly took a long, sloppy swallow of the liquor.

"Didn't lose a drop," Tim proudly proclaimed, as he smiled crookedly at his ashen faced damp fellows.

"You're a fuckin' idiot, Timmy," yelled one.

"Shit, the whole thing's gotta go now," said another, staring out at the still rocking remnants of the rusted contraption.

"What's going on Timmy?" Reinhardt asked. "Why, for the love of God, are you doing this, especially on a Wednesday night?" He immediately realized the idiocy of the question, as if the day of the week meant anything. He was actually glad to have something replace his guilt trip over lost revenue.

"It's that fucking Jean. She gave me my pin back. Tonight. That fucking bitch!" He showed everyone his fraternity pin, then threw it across the room. "Right in the stacks. Upstairs, in the graduate library. Tonight! That goddamn bitch!" He started to cry, and a couple people left the room.

They got the story in disjointed pieces, between sobs, curses, and quick pulls on the scotch bottle. His sweetheart for the past year and a half had cast him aside for a rich kid from the Phi Gam house.

"Hell, Timmy, there are plenty of broads on campus. Forget her! I know all kinds of women who would like to go out with you. You're a good-looking, funny guy. We'll help you get past this shit." Sal was sincere, but somehow his words were not resonating with his crest fallen brother.

"Everyone probably knew. Everyone but me. I'll bet you guys knew." Tim was looking at the remaining people in the room. His brown eyes were red and moist, his lips quivered, and his soaked wavy auburn hair and drenched clinging clothes gave him the appearance of a drowned rat. "How the fuck can I face anybody I know?" he blubbered.

Reinhardt, ever the logic-seeking stoic asked Tim, "Is that your main concern, or losing Jean?"

Now, everyone was gone from the room except the two ballplayers and Tim, who still sat on the floor in the middle of the room. Sal soon tired of the mumbling about hurt feelings and hating both the girl and the rich kid, and left the room.

"Christ, can you believe it?" Tim asked for at least the twelfth time. "A fucking 'Fiji'. The little cake eater! He and that bitch deserve each other."

Reinhardt sat on the floor with him. "It'll be okay, big guy. You've got a lot of good friends, and Sal's right. There are a helluva lot of girls who would like to go out with you. Sal could have you fixed up by Saturday night, I'll bet."

"I hope both you guys make the team, " Tim said, suddenly shifting the conversation to another topic, with all the usual rationale of a sot.

"It'll never happen with me," he told him. "Sal, maybe. He's good. I'm not. I'm sure I'll be cut tomorrow, and it really doesn't matter."

Then he helped his unsteady pal to his feet and down the hall to his room. As he dumped him into his bed and pulled his soaked shoes from his feet, he listened to Tim drunkenly profess their friendship to be stronger than any relationship they could possibly have with a member of the opposite sex.

"Right," he laughed as he moved a half-empty waste paper basket close to the bed and told Tim where it could be found during the night.

Tim had a cousin who played for the Cubs, and for two years he and Tim and Sal had promised they would spend some time in Chicago over the summer. It never happened, as each year they headed to their respective home cities to work tough, good paying summer jobs.

Once again, Tim started rambling about going to a Cubs game with his friends, then trailed off. "You hate the Cubs," mumbled Tim. "You like the Sox."

"Goodnight, partner." He turned off the light and quietly closed the door.

Thursday dawned clear and bright, but cold. The bad weather was swept away by a high-pressure system that left a beautiful blue sky and

58

a calm day in store. While the radio weatherman promised a warming trend by that afternoon, it felt good to wear a tie and warm pullover sweater to class under his jacket.

He did not have to cut a class to get to practice on time as he had the day before and he was surprised at how many players were on the field early, and warming up when he reached the locker room. The weatherman had nailed the prediction. It was a cool, but beautiful afternoon, with no wind and a feeling of promise in the air. He talked the assistant equipment manager out of a better fitting gray uniform. It was one that had belonged to a player cut the day before, which did not make him feel good old fashioned karma was raining down, but the uniform fit much better than his previous one. It felt good over his red-sleeved underjersey, and even added a little cockiness to his demeanor.

His confidence suffered a blow, however, when he walked out to the diamond and saw the angular, tall, blond sophomore in the outfield. He looked fast just standing still in that impeccable white home uniform, his scarlet red baseball cap set low on his forehead. The Florida flash had decided to stick around after all. He loped easily after fly balls fungoed out to him from 'Woodenhead', who was standing near the right field foul line. The outfielder was laughing and joking with the other regular players that were working near him.

"Sheep!" he thought to himself.

"What's happening, chum?" It was Sal. "C'mon, grab a ball, lets warm up."

"Looks like Joanie got it wrong for a change."

"What're you talking about?" Sal was mystified, then followed his friend's gaze out to left center. "I'm a son-of-a-bitch!" he muttered. "He's back."

"Or, he never left. Never transferred. Joanie got her wires crossed."

"I'm a son-of-a-bitch," Sal said again. "Wonder why he wasn't here yesterday?"

"I don't know, but it doesn't seem to matter to 'Woodenhead'."

Coach Woodscrim was in a great mood as he put them through a spirited workout. He kidded with several of his regulars and after fielding and base running drills, the regulars hit. Then, it was time for the non-pitching prospects, dressed in their traveling gray uniforms, to get their chance in the batting cage.

As he picked out a nice, new, white ash bottle bat to use he saw Buddy Collins walking toward him. He was sure he knew what was coming, and dropped the smooth bat and moved toward the opening in the fence near the visitors dugout.

"Where are you going?" asked Buddy as he approached the young outfielder.

"To the bench. I know what you're going to say. He's back, and you want me to sit out the swings in the cage."

Buddy looked irritated, then concerned. "You're nuts. What're you talking about?"

"The Florida 'phenom'. You've got your fill of outfielders, and he hits left-handed, and I know that's a premium this year, too."

"Look, I only wanted to tell you to be prepared to hit a little longer today. You didn't get much yesterday, but you'll get more looks today. Fernandez is trying to make the team too, and he'll be pitching to you. He'll be firing, so be ready, but go for the good pitches only. Okay? That's all I wanted to say. Stop worrying. You're getting your shot." Buddy smiled broadly at him, and he was swept by a rush of gratitude.

When he stepped into the cage he suddenly felt light, quick, swishy with the bat. The bottle bat felt as if it was an extension of his hands. The pine tar on the handle gave his hands that nice, gritty, tacky feeling that made the bat feel like a lethal weapon. The creaminess of the wood glistened in the sunlight.

"Get a good look, kid," said Sal, standing close to the cage and applying the pine tar rag to his black, heavy hickory bat.

He was the second batter that Fernandez would face, and the tall, lean pitcher was loose. He threw easily and fluidly, and his first pitch to him after he laid down the perfunctory bunts, was a straight, medium strength fastball, letter-high. He was ready for it, maybe a little too anxious, and he pulled it down the left field line. A clean double in game competition. The second pitch was just as straight, but thrown harder, and he jumped on it lining a shot over shortstop into left center.

Each of the next three pitches came in just as straight, over the heart of the plate, between the belt buckle and the letters on his uniform. He turned each pitch around with equal velocity. He hit line drives back up the middle, two off the protective screen in front of the pitcher. The third, a vicious drive into centerfield that would have taken the young right-hander's hat, and possibly his head with it, had his follow through not taken him safely behind the protective screening.

"Hooey! That's strokin' 'em, pal," hooted Sal, behind him.

Buddy Collins walked over to the pitching mound and said something to the young pitcher, who wore a worried look on his face. Buddy watched closely as Fernandez prepared to fire another pitch plateward.

Reinhardt knew a curve was coming, and he was right. He was a miserable breaking ball hitter, and decided to lay off the pitch; a wise decision as the pitch broke too soon and wound up in the dirt. He knew the young pitcher would come back with another "bender". Buddy continued to talk to the right-hander, but he continued to labor. Several more pitches missed and Woodscrim was becoming impatient. He yelled, "C'mon for crissakes, throw strikes!"

Now, the pitcher at the urging of Buddy went back to fast balls. Real grunt-wrenching, hard cheese bullets. Reinhardt popped one up, ground another between short and third, and skied one to medium right field. The last one came in thigh-high, straight down the middle, and he got all of it. Without a breeze to hinder it, or help it, the ball sailed steadily out to left center where a couple fielders started to give chase then slowed to watch it reach its apex before it dropped over the fence in the power alley. The realization that the field had suddenly grown quiet dawned on him as the pitcher pawed the earth around the mound and stared at his glove. Buddy was grinning from ear to ear, and Woodscrim stood speechless down the first base line, tobacco juice dribbling down his chin.

Sal let out a low whistle. "God damn! What'd you have for breakfast this morning? Pussy, with your cornflakes?"

"Awright, that's enough! Let's get another hitter in there." Woodscrim was back to normal.

"I've never seen you hit the ball that hard before," Sal said to him as they exchanged places in the batting cage.

"Yeah, it felt pretty good," was all he could manage before he took his place in the outfield. He never would have believed his slight frame and slender wrists could produce such power. It must be the bat, he told himself.

Sal hammered the ball also. Fernandez was done, however, and they had another pitcher who was trying to make the team pitch to him. He smashed the ball hard to all sections of the outfield, sending one over the fence down the left field line, and another off the top of the fence in straight away left field. He also drilled a very long drive to dead center field, directly between the two young men who were stationed in that vicinity.

He turned to his left, and with excellent reflexes, took off after the ball. He never noticed the tall, blond sophomore who also started after the ball. The kid from Florida had to pivot to his right and made an awkward move at the start of his pursuit, and it never gave him a chance to catch up to the other outfielder or the ball.

Reinhardt glided, then accelerated fully, always keeping the ball in sight. His spikes made a crunching sound as he landed on the crushed brick warning track, after leaping in the air and making a picture perfect, over-the-head grab of the long fly ball. His momentum carried him to the fence in center field, and he glanced at the 390 sign as he leaned on the fence momentarily before turning and lobbing the ball to another player, who congratulated him on the catch. There was nothing from the blond kid from Florida, however. Not a nod or a word. He simply returned to his original station in right center field.

"Hell," he thought to himself. "He's got it made and he knows it. I'm outta here, and he knows that too. And, he hits left-handed."

That evening at the fraternity house Sal could not stop talking about that day's practice, and how the two of them had out hustled, out worked, and out played many of the regulars. He thought they had even out done some of the players on full scholarships. When Reinhardt reminded Sal that the regulars had the team made, and did not have to work as hard as they did, his pal scoffed.

Each time he attempted to put a damper on Sal's enthusiasm, his friend dismissed his caution. Sal reminded him that only four 'wannabees' were left, and they were likely to keep three of them to flesh out the roster. Maybe all four, even if they only took sixteen or seventeen players to Savannah. At dinner, in the study room, in the television room, in their bedroom, Sal kept up the steady chatter and his overly optimistic opinions about who was likely to make the team. He was driving his roommate crazy, and the only way Reinhardt finally shut him up was to turn out the light, hop into bed, and pull the covers up over his head. Sal thought his frustration was hilarious.

Angie was a short, chunky, junior who shared his major and love of classical music. They dated each other regularly, but not exclusively. She had a cute face, with large blue eyes, a dimpled chin and little grub hands that she tried to make more elegant with false fingernails that were painted deep plum. The nails made her short, blonde hair look even lighter when she brushed it back from the sides of her face. She dressed carelessly, spoke carefully, and cared for him very much.

"Hi, Babe." He greeted her in the hallway outside one of the student union grills with a hug, and squeeze of her hand.

"Hi yourself," she answered, flashing a big grin. "How goes the battle on the athletic field?"

"Well this is Friday, 'D-Day'. Roster completion day, but let's not talk about it. Might be bad luck. I'll see you tonight at the 'Bored Boar'. We can have a few beers and something to eat, and I'll be able to tell you how everything turned out." He hesitated, then added, "My God, I hope Sal makes it. It's everything to him."

Angie pursed her lips, and studied his face intently. "What about you? How important is it for you?"

He shrugged his shoulders unconvincingly.

Athletic endeavors came up short on her barometer of important happenings on and about campus. She had watched him play rugby and thought he looked cute in those little white shorts, but did not care whether the team won or lost. She liked to drink beer with the ruggers after a game, but showed little interest in their overall success ratio. In her eyes he stood out as a renaissance man, and that was almost as important to her as international politics.

She asked if he was going to cut his last class of the day to get to practice early. When he told her yes, he had to at this juncture, she smiled wanly and said, "Good luck, if that's what you want." She did not wait for a reply, but turned and hurried away to her sociology lecture.

The practice was spirited. The regulars worked hard, hustled constantly, and kept up a regular, rhythmic chatter. They hit the ball with alarming alacrity, and appeared poised to snuff out any dwindling hopes the 'grays' may have yet held of making the team.

Counting the players left on the field several times over, he told himself that Woodscrim would keep only two of the walk-ons. Markey was in. A senior, no scholarship pending, a hard throwing pitcher, and a genuine football hero, he was in. The 'Florida flash' was back, so he obviously was going to make it. That represented two of the spots Sal had pegged as being filled by 'grays'. Maybe he would not even take two. Suddenly it mattered. It felt different to him this last 'cut' day.

His time in the cage was not productive. While not wasted, it paled by comparison with the day before. The smooth, light, bottle bat did not feel like an extension of his slender hands as it had on Thursday. It seemed to fight him.

Markey was on the mound and was throwing hard. He was wild and high on every third or fourth pitch and Woodscrim was becoming impatient, but he said nothing to him. Instead, he sent Buddy behind the pitching screen to counsel him.

Reinhardt dug in for the third time, after having been moved out of the batter's box by Markey's wildness.

He heard Sal's voice behind the cage. "C'mon, Len. He'll take something off to throw strikes. Time him. He'll groove it."

Groove it he did, with an ordinary fastball. Reinhardt turned on it beautifully, did not open up too fast, and ripped a hard line drive into left field. A clean single. Markey threw again, a faster pitch, but straight as an arrow. He hung out a frozen rope into the right center field alley, a double, possibly a triple with his speed. Now he began to feel swishy again. Loose and confident.

"Way to time it, sport," said Sal. "Watch for the bender now."

But it was not a curve; it was another belt high fastball, on the out-side corner. He was quick with the bat and caught enough of the pitch to hit it on a line between first and second and into right field. Another single.

Woodscrim made a barely perceptible gesture to Buddy, who relayed the information to Markey. He grunted as he released the next pitch. It came in high and hard, but did not break as Reinhardt expected. Bending backwards to get out of the way, his spikes caught enough dirt to make him stumble foolishly. He gingerly climbed back into the batter's box, but flexed his knees rather than dig in again. Another high and tight pitch spun him out of the box this time. Once again he planted himself, leveled the bat, and got ready for what he was sure would be a hard curve. The pitch came in with no rotation, straight at his left shoulder. He dropped flat onto his back to avoid the speeding sphere. These were 'purpose pitches' called for by the coach, and he was prepared to hang in there until he got something to swing at. Shaking and dusty, he stood in the batter's box one more time, determined to get his bat on the ball if a strike was imminent.

"Okay, that's it. Martiento, get in there!" yelled Woodscrim.

Sal's name was Maritino, and the coach knew it. He did not like Sal and his antics, and his dislike was obvious to everyone but Sal. Why he did not correct the coach when he intentionally mispro-nounced his name was unfathomable. Unless he thought by doing so he would lessen his chances of making the team. The coach seemed intent on belittling Sal, as well as changing his national heritage.

Reinhardt was quivering as he left the cage. "You rattled the big thrower. They didn't want you showin' up the big guy," said Sal, solemnly. "I'll get him for us both."

Sal got him alright. Whatever Markey threw he hit. Some shots were foul, some fair, but everything was hit hard. After Markey sat him down twice with stuff at his ribs, Sal laughed and made a quick joke, then ominously pointed his big black bat at the mound. They switched pitchers then, and Jenkins, a slender, left-handed, black kid who was trying for a second time to make the team came in to throw. He was not fast, but had great control and a lively curve ball. Sal hit him too, but not as hard, and was out in front of the lefty's off-speed pitches too often.

As Reinhardt jogged out to the outfield after having deposited his bat in the rack and retrieved his glove, Woodscrim told him, "That'll teach you to be ready, if you're going to dig in against a flame-thrower."

No one said a word to him for the balance of practice. The session ended under a mostly cloudy sky, and the late afternoon felt unseasonably warm. As they walked from the baseball field toward the locker room beyond the outfield fence, Sal explained that he had to shower and change quickly, in order to get to the main athletic office before Joanie left work. Social plans for the evening were to be mixed with an update from the grapevine.

No sooner had Sal run off to the locker room than he heard his name called. It was Coach Woodscrim walking purposefully toward him. He wanted to see him in his office in a few minutes. Before Reinhardt had a chance to say anything, Woodscrim turned on his heel, and calling to Buddy Collins, engaged the assistant coach in avid discussion. Woodscrim violated the two-foot rule when he engaged a person in intimate conversation, and Reinhardt felt particularly soiled, having been sprayed by residual tobacco juice. "How does Buddy stand it?" He wondered to himself.

After a quick shower, he turned his gray uniform, underjersey, windbreaker, and red stirrup socks in to the equipment manager. After three straight days of practice, that uniform needed laundering. The equipment manager told him to keep the scarlet red cap, whether he made the team or not.

His head was still damp when he knocked on the coach's office door. "C'mon in," yelled the hawk-faced, cranky little coach.

Depositing his books and cap on a side chair, he closed the door and took a seat on the other side of the desk from the coach.

Woodscrim wasted no time. He did not indicate whether he liked what he had seen of the young player during the three days of practice, simply told him he was keeping two of the four remaining walk-ons. He was keeping him and the left-handed pitcher, Jenkins, and now three of the players had been informed of the decision. He just had to see 'Martiento' yet.

"Maritino," Reinhardt corrected.

"What?" asked the coach, his little eyes narrowing even more.

"His name is Sal Maritino."

"Whatever," said the nasty little coach, dismissively. He looked as if he had swallowed a hunk of putrid salami.

Woodscrim then proceeded to explain that he was keeping the smallish outfielder because of his speed. They might be able to use him in certain base running situations, and as a defensive replacement in the outfield. However, he would not be making the trip south with the team, and he certainly was not getting a scholarship, and he would not be guaranteed a spot on the roster next year. If he wanted to come out for the team again, he would be welcome, along with all the other walk-ons.

Reinhardt was dumbfounded. Why was he even making the gesture? Why wasn't he taking Sal? He asked those questions of the coach, adding that it seemed to him the team needed infield help, and Sal could hit the hell out of the ball. He could see keeping the left-handed pitcher, the team needed help there, but they also needed another infielder, not an extra outfielder who would almost never play, and who would be discarded after this year.

He thought Woodscrim was going to have a stroke. He sputtered and stammered, and tobacco juice sprayed into the air, leaving little brown polka-dots all over the paperwork strewn over his messy desk.

"Are you tellin' me what I need on this team?" He was screaming, then choking on his wad of tobacco. "I've been in this game over thirty years, smart ass, and I don't need some young punk tellin' me who I should or shouldn't keep!"

Reinhardt shoved back from the desk a little more as 'Woodenhead' leaned closer to him. The polka-dots were getting closer, and he did not want them on his shirt or pants.

"I got a good mind to cut you, and keep your wise ass pal, 'Martiento'," the coach yelled.

"Maritino. His name is Salvatore Maritino. He's from Syracuse, New York, in case you're interested."

"That's it," exploded Woodscrim. "You're done, buster. Get your goddamn things and get out of my office!"

As he nervously picked up his books and hat, he kept a watchful eye on the irate little coach. He honestly thought he might take a swing at him.

"Buddy!" screamed Woodscrim. "Get in here!"

The assistant coach opened the door almost instantly. Woodscrim told him to send 'Martiento' in to see him. When told that Sal was not in the locker room, the coach went ballistic all over again, kicking a waste paper basket, and throwing a book on hitting techniques against the wall.

"I know where he is. I'll get him for you," Reinhardt said, gently squeezing past Buddy Collins, and out of the coach's office.

Buddy quickly closed the door on the swearing, spitting coach whose last decipherable words were, "And leave that goddamn hat with the equipment manager."

"Fuck you, 'Woodenhead'," he muttered, as he carefully placed his baseball hat over his still damp hair.

He told Buddy that Sal was at the athletic office, and he would leave immediately to get him. He told the assistant coach that he would ask Sal to see him first, as he wanted Buddy to talk with him before he sent him in to see the head coach. "Tell him he's a sheep."

"What?" asked Buddy.

"Just tell him he's a sheep, before you send him in to see Woodscrim. Okay?"

"I don't understand," said Buddy, looking more confused than he usually did. "I never understand you."

"Trust me. Sal will know what you're talking about. Don't say anything else. The coach will tell him the rest."

"Okay. Just go get him now, before the old man has another fit," said Buddy. "I'll remember. He's a sheep."

"Right." He smiled, and turned to leave the locker room.

Cows in the Alley

She told her sister Mary that Mr. Grunhoff had spit on her leg in the balcony of the local theatre. Her sister asked if she thought he had done it on purpose, but before she could answer, her sister rushed on, insisting he could not have done such a thing with premeditation. Her older sister, and her best friend, often answered questions for her. Indeed, she quite often expressed opinions for the both of them, without consulting her. She fully accepted and expected her older sister's assertions.

"No, he couldn't have meant it," she reaffirmed, meaninglessly. "He was trying to spit his tobacco juice to the side, and I don't think he was aiming for me."

She cringed, and Mary laughed, as she recounted how the stream had landed on her calf with a 'splot', and made her cotton stocking begin to sag as it ran down into her shoe. She said it started to make her sick, and she wanted to run to the ladies room.

"Why didn't you?" asked Mary.

"Because he might have noticed what he did."

"And you didn't want him to know he spit on you?" Her older sister was incredulous. "How silly. He didn't do it on purpose, so why did you just sit there and feel sick?"

She did not have an answer. She thought her sister might provide one. Then she quickly shifted the conversation to what the film had been about, and what girls were there with her. She found the star, William S. Hart, attractive, and mentioned that he was considered handsome and dashing by her friends, and that the western had been tremendously exciting. The afternoon at the Imperial had been enjoyable, notwithstanding her tobacco juice-soaked stockings.

Her older sister rebuked and corrected her. "William S. Hart is **not** handsome. He's a cowboy. Who likes cowboys, anyhow?"

"I do," she said. "My friends do too. You only like Mary Pickford."

"She's a great actress. Everyone likes Mary Pickford."

"She's okay, but you only like her because she's got the same name."

"What's wrong with that?" Mary stared straight into her younger sister's eyes. Even though she was three years younger, they were almost the same height. Mary was cute, petite, and wore a huge, floppy bow in her hair, which she continually fluffed and fretted over. She liked to challenge her younger sister, who was rather plain, raw boned, introspective and insecure. She considered her to be uninteresting and never a match for her wits.

"Nothing. But, I have a right to like cowboy pictures."

"That's stupid," said Mary, cutting off any further discussion about last Saturday's activities. "Mom gives you the afternoon off, and you go see William S. Hart. C'mon, we're gonna be late," and she fluffed the bow and tossed her hair.

Their conversation took place where so many of their meaningful discourses as well as sisterly spats usually did, in the alley behind the main street that ran through the heart of their immigrant neighborhood. They hurried on the cobblestones to their school, St. Athanasius, where they were taught by the Notre Dame nuns. She kept looking behind her until they reached the end of the alley where they would turn right and walk three more blocks to their school.

"What's the matter?" asked Mary, clearly irritated.

"We beat the cows today," she replied in a relieved voice.

"No," responded her sister. "We're late. I bet the cows have already been through."

"I don't think so," she said quietly, yet quite sure of herself. "We haven't seen any cow droppings. We'd have stepped in a cow pie by now." She looked back one more time at the narrow alley that was only dimly lit by the early May morning sunshine.

Mary did not respond. That was a clear sign she was right, and she trailed her older sister, feeling triumphant for the next three blocks.

This was to be her older sister's last year at the Catholic school. In another month, when school let out, she would be through with the critical nuns and their hounding, vituperative ways. Their father had already made the decision that Mary would work part-time while attending a vocational school for two years starting in the fall, before going to work on a full-time basis. She worried that her relationship with her older sister would be forever changed, as their walks to school, their whispered secrets in the alley would cease in four short weeks. Her sister was already spending much of her free time with two older girls, sisters from two streets away who attended the vocational school. The oldest, fifteen and flirtatious, would be employed at a factory that made women's corsets in less than a month. She was finishing her schooling, and her father already had the job arranged for her. Mary admired her and found spending time with her to be exciting and dangerous, as the older girl explained what life at the vocational school would be like. She was also quite explicit about her relations with neighborhood boys, and how best to utilize feminine charm to attract suitors and improve grades in school.

"You like the Kaffler girls a lot, don't you?" she asked her older sister one morning as they walked through the alley. "You like Gretchen the most."

Mary barely glanced at her as she responded, "Yes. They're nice girls. Gretchen knows everything, and she gives us advice."

"Do you like her the best?"

Mary knew what she was angling for, reassurance that she would not forget her when she left the elementary school and embarked on new challenges. Her younger sister wanted to be soothed, and told that they would still be able to share secrets. But she would not offer her that affirmation. Instead, she simply said, "I like Gretchen a lot. She's older and smarter, and the boys all like her."

"You like her the best, 'cause she's the oldest?"

Her sister did not respond because their conversation was interrupted by the sudden thunderous sounds of hooves on the cobblestones behind them. They shrieked and ran the rest of the way to the end of the alley and glanced around the corner when they reached safety, to watch the advancing small herd of beef cattle being driven to a local packing house by two men wielding long metal poles.

"Here come the cows," she said needlessly to her sister. It was an almost daily occurrence that formed a core of their morning routine. It was anticipated by her as much as talking about private matters with her older sister, and as such, gave assurance that life would proceed in predictable fashion. She did not like surprises.

Gretchen and her sister were at their house on a Saturday afternoon, and she heard them talking about mysterious things with Mary. Gretchen and Mary whispered and snickered about some girl who had been attending the vocational school until recently and then had left the neighborhood quickly to live with an aunt on the east side of the city. On Monday, in the alley on the way to school, she asked her older sister about that conversation.

"Oh, she went to live with relatives 'cause she's gonna have a baby," said Mary.

"I thought you had to be married to have a baby."

"No, Gretchen said she was gonna have a 'baxter'," said Mary authoritatively.

"What's a 'baxter'?"

"Shh, lower your voice!" her older sister said quickly, looking around nervously. "It's not something people talk about."

"Well, I never heard of it," she insisted. "If she's not married, and she's gonna have a baby, how'd that happen?"

"Well, silly, that's why they call it a 'baxter'. That's what Gretchen called it. It's not proper. She was messing around with boys, and she and Gretchen would show them their breasts, and I guess that's when it happened, and now she's gone away to live."

The young girl was very puzzled now. "Why would they show their breasts to boys?"

"I don't know. Gretchen says boys like to see 'em, and she says she likes to show 'em off." She was becoming annoyed with her younger sister, and wanted to end the conversation since she was not sure of the facts and reasons herself.

Her sister persisted however, stopping in the middle of the alley when they still had a couple blocks to traverse before they made their right turn. "But what's that got to do with the baby?"

"It's a 'baxter' I told you," shouted Mary angrily, then looked around quickly before walking away from her open-mouthed, confused sister.

She stood there watching her older sister quickly retreat from her, when she heard the hooves. She glanced back and saw them advancing in the gloomy distance. "Here come the cows!" She ran swiftly and caught up with her sister as they turned the corner, laughing and breathlessly planning the rest of the day's activities.

Typical of the workings of a child's mind, the discussion and confusion it created for her was forgotten the following day. As they quickly walked the length of the alley during the start of a soggy day, she listened to Mary describe the whipping their brother, Franz, was going to get from their father for staying out too late the night before. He then compounded the problem by leaving the house early that morning to avoid the wrath of their father.

"How come Papa almost never talks to Mama?" She asked Mary the question while her older sister was in mid-sentence.

"Why do you ask me questions like that? That isn't even what I was talking about," her sister said impatiently.

"Well, it just seems like he talks to us kids, but he never talks to Mama. Maybe he's unhappy, and that's another reason why he's always gonna beat the boys."

"If he and Mama are unhappy, it isn't 'cause of us kids. Unless they don't have enough money, and maybe that's because they got five kids." Mary sounded smug, then quickly changed her tone to one of a questioning nature. Her sister watched her closely. She was rethinking her statements.

"How come Papa talks German to us, but he only wants us to answer him in English?"

Mary considered this question carefully before answering. "I think it's because of the war."

"What war?"

"The war that just ended a couple years ago, you dunce!" said Mary irritably. She looked at her sister as if she had cockroaches crawling out of her nose. "You're a baby. You don't remember anything. We fought the Kaiser, and won."

"What's that got to do with Papa not wanting us to talk German at home?"

Her older sister was exasperated. "He doesn't want us to talk German 'cause we beat the Germans. He wants everyone to know we're Americans and not Germans. So, he wants us to only talk English." She hesitated, and her younger sister could tell she was thinking deeply. "Maybe that's why we don't hear him talking to Mama. His English isn't good, so he just doesn't talk much."

"But he talks to us kids. Anyhow, we're Austrians, not Germans."

Mary looked closely at her sister and wondered how she would ever grow up, how she would last on her own at St. Athanasius. She wanted to say something to her that would put everything right, that would answer all her questions. Instead, she slowly shook her head in frustration, and roughly pinched her sister's arm, causing her to scream. They began to run as it rained harder.

The closing days of the school year went too quickly for her. She dreaded the coming summer when Mary would spend all of her time with the Kaffler sisters and other girls with whom she would be attending vocational school. She wondered how much Mary would change in the coming months. One lazy evening flooded by a late May sunset she trailed her sister and the Kafflers as they walked home from the Imperial. They had watched the posting of signs of the coming attractions, and Gretchen had flirted with several boys hanging around the local theatre and burlesque house. She heard Gretchen describe how she allowed one of them to play with her in a darkened hallway, and how he had said her breasts were beautiful. When they were home, Mary told her not to repeat anything she had heard to anyone. She promised she would not, but she asked her sister if she would start showing her breasts to boys once she started attending the vocational school. Mary laughed and said she doubted that she would. She was relieved, but she made Mary promise to go to confession if she did.

The last day of school was warm and sunny, and while most of the children squirmed in their seats, anxious to flee the dismal brick edifice, she had to bite her lower lip to keep from crying. She hated change and confusion, and everything was going to be different in her life and in school from now on. The nun that had taught her class for the past year made a startling announcement right after lunch that was greeted by cheers and clapping by only a few students, her pets in the classroom. She would teach a different grade level next term and they would have her as their teacher again.

She stared at the tall angular nun with the narrow, dark, mean eyes, and felt terrible. Her eyes were moist and her stomach ached. Most of the children were silent and glanced nervously about themselves, but she could only think that this was one change she had looked forward to, and now it would not happen. She would have to endure another year of a nun who ridiculed her, and she would not have Mary to accompany her every morning. She told this to her sister on their way home as she studied the dark windows and doorways of the alley. She wanted the images of everything that last day of school to remain vividly in her mind, to carry everything over to the next school year.

Mary assured her that everything would be fine, that they would still have quiet talks and shared secrets in the evening after supper. She promised her younger sister that she would always be willing to listen to her problems and answer her questions, and tried to ease her mind by suggesting that maybe something would happen to that nun over the summer. Maybe she would have a different teacher in the fall. The ungainly sibling smiled at her older sister, now that she had some hope of redemption.

They were holding hands and swinging their arms when she asked her older sister again about their parents' inability to communicate.

Mary faced her sister and said, "You're too worried about them not being happy. Why wouldn't they be happy? Papa doesn't like any-thing to change, just like you, and nothing ever changes in his life."

"Change scares me. Maybe it scares Papa, too."

"Look, sometimes change is good," said Mary, forcing herself to stay calm and speak slowly to her younger sister, even though she was becoming impatient. "One day you'll be grown up, and everything will change then. You won't always go to school and live at home."

She thought about this as they finished their walk in the alley, and was preparing another question for her sister when Mary suddenly let go of her hand and turned in the opposite direction from their street.

"Where are you going?"

"I have to meet Gretchen when she gets home from work. I'm going to her house to wait for her with her sister. She's gonna tell us all about her new job," said Mary.

"Can I come too?"

"No, you better go home. Mama will be looking for you. Tell her I won't be long, and I'll do my chores as soon as I get home."

"She might be mad."

Mary laughed and said, "That's okay, she won't stay mad long. She knows things will be different after this summer, when I go to vocational school. See? That'll be a change, too. You worry too much, silly." She fingered her large bow and abruptly turned away.

She watched her older sister walk down the street, humming to herself, her hips moving with an exaggerated swinging movement.

She wiped her tears with her sleeve, and realized that they had not seen the cows that morning.

Swimming from Washington

The train was stalled at Washington Street and he was late. It had started badly when he woke up with a headache, fell back to sleep, got up late and missed his normal bus. After ten minutes on the sweltering subway car, and several indecipherable announcements by the conductor on why they were in a holding pattern, he got off and sprinted up the stairs into the blinding Chicago July sun.

He hustled down Dearborn, and noticed a flashing sign that alternated time and temperature. Not quite nine o'clock and it was eighty-five degrees. He should have slowed down, but did not, and by the time he reached his office on Jackson Boulevard his shirt was soaked through and his suit coat was moist from being carried. Casimir Matuska was still breathing heavily as he stepped from the elevator when it stopped it the twentieth floor.

Hot as it was, he poured himself a cup of coffee from the marketing department's automatic coffee maker and carried it into his office. He had just loosened his tie and was going through the mail stacked neatly in the middle of his desk when Jeannie, the department's supervising administrative assistant, stuck her head in and asked, "You didn't forget the meeting with the folks from the radio station, did you?"

"No, I didn't forget," he lied. "I just had to come into the office for something I forgot last night. The mix is at ten, right?"

"Yes. Over at the Whitman Studio on Michigan. Wow, you look rough. Why are you so damp?"

"The train stopped at Washington. I couldn't wait, so I walked down."

"Tough night?"

"Tough and late," he said, rubbing his forehead as he searched his center drawer for aspirin. "I was out late with that Browning guy, the one who owns all those stores in the Sacramento Valley."

Jeannie laughed and said, "That's what advertising managers get paid for, right?"

"Right." He glanced at his watch, gathered some papers into his briefcase and headed for the door. "I'll be back after the meeting and mix. My dictation is in the bin, and the filing is on the corner of my desk. And would you please ask Angie to rough up a letter of intro to that small chain in Denver? Use the boilerplate and I'll look it over when I get back. I'd have done it myself, but right now I'm busier than a bulldog on a cat farm."

"No problem," she said. "Good luck with Mr. Fox."

That brought him up short. "What? Is he going to be there?"

"Apparently. He told me yesterday that he wouldn't be in this morning; that he was going right to Whitman. And he'd be in after that."

"Hell, he never said anything to me. I wonder why he wants to be there?"

Jeannie paused, pursed her lips, then added quietly, "I don't think he's happy about the costs involved. I think he's getting heat about production costs."

"Thanks for the 'heads-up', Jeannie," he said appreciatively.

She smiled at him and gave his arm a gentle squeeze. She was a smart, attractive young woman, with dark hair and eyes, and busy breasts that never seemed to be fully contained in her bra. She was a true 'go to' girl for him and John Corrigan, the firm's sales manager. She liked overseeing the secretaries that worked for the two 'wild men' of the food company's marketing department, and they liked working with her also. They could toss any project at her and she could coordinate it with the company's clerical staff and get it done right, the first time. She also provided valuable intelligence reports, because she disliked and mistrusted their boss of the past six months, Rodney Fox, as much as they did.

Rodney Fox had been brought in as Vice President of marketing of N. A. F. E., a large food processor, to increase sales and cut costs. A neat trick, if you could do it in tangible products. His father-in-law was C.E.O., but of course nepotism had nothing to do with it. He replaced Fred Torrey, who had been with the firm over 35 years, was everybody's friend, and Cas' own personal mentor. He was the gentleman who had hired him over fifteen years ago. When Fred retired early, everyone felt the loss, but not as much as Cas had.

"Hello Matty!" It was his partner in crime, the irrepressible John Corrigan calling to him from his office, as he walked through the marketing department on his way to the elevators. Late as he was he could not resist a little bantering with his close friend and fellow manager.

"What's up, 'Wrong Way'?" he asked as he stepped into the sales manager's disheveled, cluttered office, filled with baseball memorabilia. John was a large, overweight, gregarious Northsider. At forty-seven, he was two years younger than the advertising manager, but they were both long-term employees of the Exchange, as the company was referred to. Both had grown up in the food business. John wore outrageous ties with striped shirts, suspenders, and a perpetual grin. He had a shock of dark hair that he incessantly had to brush from his forehead, and hands like hams, which he used to thump his buddies on the back in a familial fashion. Nothing pleased the sales manager more than having chili for breakfast at 5:00 a.m. following an afternoon of golf and an all-night foray into various pubs with his buddies, and Matuska was his principal playmate. Corrigan's wife, Melanie, allowed him to get away with far too much, but only if she knew Matuska was going to be around to shepherd her wayward husband home.

"Not too much, Matty," said John, grinning as he shoved the latest sales figures from the eastern region across the desk at his friend. "Those new stores we're in are doing well. We're moving food like mad in the Pittsburgh area. Right in the teeth of the enemy. Geez, what happened to you? You look like you got dressed in the shower."

"I had to swim to the office, from Washington Street. Listen, Johnny, me boy, I'd love to stay and take copious notes on your epistle on how to sell mustard in the land of ketchup, but I'm late for a re-record on Michigan, and 'da man' gonna be there."

"Hey, that's twice in the last month he's sat in on your client meetings, isn't it?"

"Three times. I'm really starting to feel antsy. He doesn't like me, and he doesn't see the need for the advertising department."

"That's nuts! He doesn't like anyone. Don't take it personally. And, what the hell would he do without an advertising manager? He couldn't oversee it himself. What's he gonna do, give it to the sales department?" Saying that, Corrigan motioned widely about his disorganized office, replete with paperwork stacked in three of the four corners.

"You never know, J.C."   He started for the door when Corrigan came around his desk and clapped a ham-fisted hold around his shoulders.

"You take care of yourself, Matty. Don't back up, but watch your goddamned mouth. Don't dig yourself a hole, either. Just remind him who you are and what you do for this frigging place. Remember, he came from a paper manufacturer. What's he know about canned pineapple?"

"Absolutely! I'm Cas Matuska, and I are a advertiser!"

The two friends walked together to the elevators, and John Corrigan asked him, "Hey, you wanna come for brunch on Sunday? Melanie said to ask you, and the kid's been asking about her 'Uncle Matty'. I think I can rustle us up a couple tickets to the Cubs game, too. We can eat and run, Melanie will use it as an opportunity to go to her mom's for the day."

"Yeah, love to, at least for the meal and to see your lovely wife and daughter, but don't work too hard on the tickets. I don't give a shit about watching the Cubs. Go Sox!" He stepped into the elevator and laughed at his friend who was giving him the finger as the doors closed.

The sound studio was refreshingly cool, and there were donuts and fresh coffee on a side table. He helped himself to a glazed twist and a cup of black coffee, and took it over to a small round table in the corner.

The idea was to use the old soundtrack on the grocery chain's advertising tape, background music and all, and mix it with a new voice over. The chain, a Southern Plains company that specialized in many of the brands N. A. F. E. produced, had always relied on the clout and production experience of the food producer. They wanted a different voice this year, however. One with a more believable, near South twang.

The announcer he chose was local but was born in Southwestern Missouri. He really wanted someone from Dallas or Tulsa or Oklahoma City, but this young guy was good, and cheap.

The producer from the ad agency they used on this project was a busy little fellow with owl-like glasses. He was short, scrawny, nervous and wore a bow tie. A bow tie, when it was ninety degrees!

"Hi Matty," he said when he saw the advertising manager. "Your boss said to tell you he wanted to see you at the far end of the hall, when you came in." He was a little too pleased to give Matuska this message.

"Great," thought Cas Matuska. "Now I'm taking orders from fag producers. The son-of-a-bitch really does want me out."

He listened to several lines from the announcer, and told the producer to tell him where to use 'throw away' lines.

"I beg your pardon." The little producer was offended. He was the expert. Why should he have to listen to the client's representative? "He's very close. I just want him to accentuate the closing."

"No, don't have him do that," said Matuska. "I hired him because of where he's from, and for the natural nasal quality in his voice. That's what the chain wants. If he hits the last line too hard, he won't sound natural."

"I think I can decide what sounds more natural," said the producer in a huff.

"He doesn't need to hear what's 'natural'. Just have him throw the last line away, in his own laid back style," said Matuska as he started down the hallway. "What would you know about 'natural', anyway?" thought the advertising manager.

"You're late," said an unsmiling Rodney Fox, as Matuska entered the small combination office-meeting room. His boss sat at a table with Arnie Roberts, the diminutive director of advertising for the grocery chain they were trying to please. If they could please Arnie, he did not care what the advertising venture would cost, because he and his chain would place a lot more orders with the food processor. Arnie liked working with him, and seemed uncomfortable sitting there with Fox.

"Sorry, I was in the studio listening to the announcer lay down a few tracks. I think he's what you want, Arnie."

"You're still late," said Fox, shifting into his intimidating schoolmaster's tone. He was a short, dapper little man, with a neatly trimmed mustache and thinning blond hair still worn in a rather old fashioned way, casually parted in the middle so it flowed evenly to either side. At forty-six, he was viewed as the wunderkind of the company. He carried himself with ramrod precision and walked with crisp, short, mincing movement. Because of who he was related to in the company, he exhibited an air of invincibility. Arnie felt uncomfortable during the meeting; he sensed the tension between the two men, and indicated a willingness to spend more money on next year's advertising budget. This year was a different matter, as his budget was cast in stone. Fox did not hide his disdain for the small, self-deprecating advertiser, mostly because of his obvious friendship with Matuska. After several futile attempts to alter the advertising schedule and material, Arnie left the studio feeling hurt and betrayed.

On their way back to the lobby, Matuska mentioned to Fox that he wanted to check on the tracks that were laid down by the announcer. The mix would be completed and transferred to another type of tape and then disc, before the day was out. He listened to a couple and discussed them with the producer. One seemed perfect, but the producer demurred because Cas obviously preferred it. Before the haggling grew anymore intense, Fox interjected, told the producer to make the choice, and suggested to Matuska that they have lunch before returning to the office.

Rodney Fox left the studio and headed up Michigan Avenue in brisk fashion, with his chin resolutely tucked into the perfect knot of his perfect foulard tie. Matuska normally walked fast, but he was a step behind the agitated Mr. Fox.

"Busy, busy! Well fuck you!" thought Matuska, as perspiration began to pool around the back of his waistband. "If you want to sweat like a horse, go ahead, but I've had my exercise for the day."

They hailed a cab and Fox directed the driver to take them to a snooty, English style tavern and restaurant off Ontario. A very dark, cool place, with an over abundance of polished mahogany and shiny brass trim. Conversation in the place was as muted as the little bit of color the room held.

"Cas, who are you?" Rodney Fox asked him the question straight out, with no small talk, after their drinks were served.

Matuska considered the question at length, as he looked straight into Fox's unblinking, icy blue eyes. He was nervous, and bit lightly on his lower lip, then thought, "The hell with it. I'll play it straight up with the bastard. He and I are never going to get along anyway."

"Well Rodney," he started slowly, drawing the name out, because he knew that Fox preferred to be called 'Rod', then built into a nice rhythm, "I'm just a South side Polish kid, born and bred in the city. Lucky enough to go to private schools, even college. I think I work hard, and I like what I do. I party pretty hard too, which I'm sure you're aware of. I try to dress nicely, and to speak and write well. I tell the truth, love my family, and hate the traffic in this town. I have a divorce under my belt, a nice condo on the northwest side, a receding hairline, and a five-year old convertible that runs when it feels like it. Oh, and most people call me 'Matty', so feel free."

"We've talked before, Cas," said Fox pointedly, "And I'm not sure you've heard everything I've said. That's why I asked you who you were. I thought you might tell me what you're about."

He lost Matuska completely at that point, but the advertising manager was not going to give him the satisfaction of looking confused. They had previously discussed most of the information he had just spouted. Instead, he leaned back in his chair and put his hands together, steeple-like, and pressed them against his pursed lips. He wanted to appear engrossed, but with the aura of a sphinx.

Fox continued. "I've looked closely at your personnel file. You're well educated, Northwestern and such, and you rose through the ranks in rather rapid fashion. I'd say you were even cunning in the way you helped Fred Torrey replace your predecessor with you five years ago. That took ingenuity. Not that those details are in your file, but I've talked with enough people to know that you're sharp, read situations quickly, and can recognize opportunity when it knocks."

Now Matuska leaned forward, and placed his hands on the table. "What does Fred Torrey have to do with this?"

"Nothing, but you apparently convinced him that the advertising area needed sprucing up, and your predecessor retired four years early. Correct?"

Matuska did not respond, but his nervousness was being overtaken by anger.

Fox continued. "I don't believe advertising is necessary in our organization anymore. Not in its current set-up. The question is whether the company should pick up the cost on this venture today, or any other such advertising expenditure." He was talking rapidly now, but he still had that glossed over veneer that made him seem like he never perspired, and was always in control. Matuska, on the other hand, felt his shirt sticking to his back, and he wanted to remove his jacket.

"Cas, I have figures that I can show you that will prove advertising in our corporation is costing us money, not adding to sales. There is no other way to put it. Some advertising is good, it's necessary, but the way you're running things is proving to be a straight drain on revenue."

"Rodney, if you want to dump advertising, I'm sure you'll suggest to the board that it be done post-haste. Why bring up my past work with the company? I can defend my position, but I don't think you're interested."

"I'm very interested," said Fox, as he pulled a carefully creased paper from his inside jacket pocket. "I have here a detailed accounting report on your last trip to Minneapolis. To say the least, you entertain very well. Care to review with me your last business dinner in town?"

"Did you happen to notice the sizeable order that came in from the client the following month?"

"Apples and oranges, Cas. We're not talking about one for one in dollars spent."

Now Cas was exercised, and he stated a little too loudly, "Hell no it isn't dollar for dollar. What I'm spending is a pittance. I'm giving them good, solid information, and damn smart advertising help. I'm not buying their affection. Look at their sales orders over the past three years."

Fox gave him a smarmy look, as he leaned back. "Because you're bright and you know the business is why I wanted to talk about your past experience with the company. No one seems to be minding the store in advertising, and in its current form as I stated before, it's a drain on the operation, but you could find other challenges in the company. I'm transferring advertising to Corrigan in sales. Advertising will answer to sales, and I'm bringing in Jeff Carrow to administer whatever corporate advertising we do in the future."

Matuska sat there dumbfounded. He found himself saying, "Carrow's in production. What does he know about advertising?"

"He has a degree in advertising from Iowa. He's a smart kid, and we feel he's being underutilized."

"Well, what exactly am I supposed to do? What challenges do you have in mind?" He wondered if his face was red. He felt hot and flushed, and his hand shook as he took a drink of his coffee.

Rodney Fox waved the waiter away dismissively, as he told him they were not ready to order lunch yet. "I've gotten clearance to beef up research and development."

Fred Torrey hated research and development. He felt that was part of sales, but since Fox had come on board, it had taken on a life of its own, and was currently staffed by two recent college grads and a full-time clerical person.

"Research and development," said Matuska, dumbly. "Wow. That doesn't sound like much. It could get boring, with three people doing whatever they do down there."

"There won't be three, Cas. We're transferring Fran Leland to distribution, in Milwaukee. She's very eager to do something else. You know, like you. Learn the business from ground zero. So, it'll be you and Irene Cruz in 'R & D'."

"That's it? Do I get a choice? Isn't there something else you can offer me? What about the heads of other divisions, don't they have something?" I'm not eager to do anything else. I like what I do." He tried not to sound desperate, but knew he did. His voice was trying to outrace his feverish brain, and he felt like a deer caught in the head-lights of a truck.

"There's nothing else, Cas," said Fox, smiling like a crocodile zero-ing in on a frog. "We've discussed the figures in the boardroom. Everyone agrees. You know how you got the job, well, you've cer-tainly had to prepare yourself to lose it in much the same way."

"What have I done to make you hate me?"

"You sound sophomoric, Cas. Let's stick to the central issue, okay?"

"You know Fred Torrey would have never gone along with something like this," began Matuska, trying a different tact, when Fox cut him off abruptly, putting a hand up like a stop sign for emphasis.

"To repeat your thought, Cas, what does Fred Torrey have to do with this? Fred is gone, you're here, and you'll have to fight this one on your own."

"Just what am I supposed to say? What am I supposed to do around the Exchange now, except for working for a kid in 'R & D'?"

"What do you think you should do?"

"I think," said Matuska carefully, "that I've just been invited to resign."

"Cas, if you feel that the situation is intolerable; that you cannot offer anything meaningful to the company anymore, I'll respect any decision you make. I'm not asking you to resign. No one at the firm is. I want to make that perfectly clear."

"Jesus," thought Matuska. "The bastard even looks like Nixon!"

"Advertising is to be transferred to sales in four weeks, after we clear up the last details of the contracts we still have pending," said Fox. "You have until that time to decide whether you want the transfer. We have nothing else for you after that, if you don't want research and development."

"Does anyone else know about this?" asked Matuska. "How about Corrigan, what does he say?"

"No one knows but the board and the division heads. John Corrigan will be told at the end of the week by official written notice, as well as at the weekly marketing meeting. Now, let's order lunch."

He slid into the gracious host mode in such an oily fashion it made Matuska feel useless and worthless. "No thanks," he said as he stood up. "I'm not hungry. Thanks for the coffee."

He started for the door, then returned to the table. "I'm not a kid. Where will I go, what will I do?" He immediately despised himself for showing weakness.

"Don't make a hasty decision, Cas," said Rodney Fox, smiling easily. "Think about it, and we'll talk prior to the marketing meeting. I know this has been sudden, but it's right for the company. It's a dog eat dog world."

"Other way around in my world, Rodney."

Still smiling with smug satisfaction, Fox asked, "Perhaps I should ask you why you hate me so much. You do, don't you, Cas?"

"Your words, Rodney, my sentiment."

He was not quite sure what had happened. His head was spinning as he blinked his eyes in the hot, steamy, blinding Chicago sun. He wondered if Fox wanted him out just because of the expense of the advertising department, or because this was an excuse to dump someone he did not care for and thought he would not be able to work with. Whatever the reason, it would be an opportunity for Fox to ease more of his kind of people into positions of influence and to closely control those he did not trust. God, he hated the guy. Cas had the reputation, because of how he had gained his position, of being a fun loving, good-natured, but ruthless individual. But, this guy was a career-ender, an assassin.

"I ought to quit," thought Matuska. "The asshole wants me out and just insulted me, and treated the whole thing like he was dumping day old coffee grounds."

No, he knew better. You do not quit and look for a job. You get another job first, then quit. Hell, he also knew he would quit within the next four weeks, whether he had another job or not.

"What I ought to do is waste the son-of-a-bitch," thought Matuska. "I could spend a few hundred and have Dommie talk to a couple of the lads and have him 'offed'. No, I'd rather grease his ass myself."

Sunday afternoon found him at Wrigley Field with his good friend, John Corrigan. They had upper deck reserved seats, but they were not paying much attention to the Cardinals' slaughter of the Cubs on the field. They drank a lot of beer and talked about what was discussed two days earlier in the marketing meeting. The usually funny, engaging Corrigan was somber. He was concerned about his friend, who had told him on the train ride to the ballpark that he was going to tender his letter of resignation within the next couple weeks. Cas had also told him of his wild fantasy of execution. For the fifth time in an hour he asked him, "Are you sure, Matty? You sure you want to jump ship right now?"

"Good Lord willin', and the creek don't rise, 'Wrong Way'!"

"I'm worried about you, buddy. You worry me, and I'm serious. You wouldn't really have him 'whacked', would you?" Corrigan's tongue was getting thick. Matuska thought he was funnier than usual when he had a few drinks.

"Things happen for the best, 'Wrong Way'," said Mauska as he signaled for the Old Style beer man. "Change is good. It's good for all parties concerned. You'll have what's left of advertising. Dom will have some extra cash. Little Hitler will have hell now, and I'll be able to visit him later, when I get there"

"Shit. We'll never see each other. Things won't be the same," said Corrigan, getting too serious now to suit Matuska. "I'll be left alone to deal with that bastard."

"Not if he's dead."

"I'm serious, Cas. Nobody's going to get killed, but you'll be gone." Corrigan hesitated, and Matuska was afraid his friend would start crying. "Shit. I'm all fucked up right now. I'll be alone."

"I don't think so, pal," said Matuska. "There are others that see him for what he is. Just watch yourself. Be careful with whom you share ideas. And, we **will** see each other. I'm not the one who's dying, unless you know something I don't."

After a long silence and three more Cardinal runs, Corrigan said he was going to use the restroom, and that he would bring two more Old Styles back with him.

Cas Matuska sighed and thought it funny that it would end this way. No testimonials. No gold watch. No fireworks. You just got drunk in the upper deck, watching a home team you don't even care about.

Major Magnolia

The Kentucky fog was burned off by the October sun, leaving only small damp spots on the pavement near the hotel. Leaves dripped intermittently with the last vestiges of that morning's moisture.

Taxi cabs arrived and departed with a certain urgency spurred on by a policeman's whistle and the motions and frantic calls of the hotel's doormen. Jockeying drivers leaned out to exchange unpleasantries that mercifully remained incomprehensible to their passengers.

Angela was one of the last in the current lineup of guests to get a cab. She thought she had been suitably dressed when she left her room, but now felt slightly chilled, as the remaining damp crept upward through her fashionably sensible shoes.

A young, immaculately dressed business woman was also on her own. Angela eyed her with distrust if not distaste. She carried an exquisite Gucci leather bag that perfectly matched her oxblood pumps. The bag must have doubled as her briefcase, and Angela wondered what was in it in addition to important papers. Necessary, sensible things most probably: A palm pilot, aspirin, midol, gold Cross pen, calendar, clean linen handkerchief, small spray of CK? She looked so confident, so successful, so imperious, so young, that Angela began working herself up into a hatred of this young woman, who seemed to be everything that she herself was not. She imagined the woman to be constantly flooded with social invitations and romantic overtures, while her own love life, if that is what one could label it, consisted of a short lived, failed marriage, that resulted in an insolent, insecure daughter. Her usual, unkind, critical and hateful thoughts of her daughter crowded her mind as she studied the young stranger. Did one remind her of the other?

They shared what appeared to be the last cab. Who knew how long until the next horde would queue up?

Not quite condescending, but exhibiting an ego that was definitely well fed, the young, well heeled, woman coolly thanked her for sharing, and indicated she was headed to a meeting in Lansdowne, and then inquired where Angela might be let off.

The cab was heading southeast on Main, and Angela suddenly had the urge to jump from the moving vehicle. She insisted they had gone far enough for her convenience, and virtually leaped from the car when it stopped near Ashland Avenue. She threw more than enough money onto the woman's lap to cover her fare for her relatively short ride, and mumbled something to the effect of 'covering tip' before slamming the car door with such velocity that it could only be interpreted as 'get going' by the driver.

He did. With squealing tires, he blasted back into moderately heavy late morning traffic, and she started her leisurely walk up Main Street. Past stores, restaurants, and apartments, where Main turned into Richmond Road, and widened and grew leafy and colorful, she walked and began to marvel at the change in architecture. Removing her cardigan and glancing at the suddenly cloudless sky, she was thankful she had not retreated to her hotel room for more, or warmer clothes.

The mansions, some remade into offices or multi-family dwellings, grew larger, grander, more exquisite as she continued her eastward trek. It had been at least six years since she had visited Lexington, yet it remained so familiar, so pretty, so quintessentially old South, she half expected to meet Henry Clay himself coming towards her.

Instead, it was her cousin, Beth. She thought she would be early, so she had walked more slowly than usual, or maybe she walked farther than she anticipated. No mind, they were together, hugging each other as they stood on the narrow sidewalk outside the handsome brick Georgian colonial shaded by several huge, old trees.

"Did you just arrive?" Beth asked her.

"Yes. Of course. Where else would I have been?" She laughed at the absurd question.

"Well, you might have walked around the neighborhood. It's so pretty today, and you could have been early, and since I wasn't here, I thought you might have been by this way at least once before."

"No," Angela laughed again. " I just got here."

"This is it," Beth said, motioning towards the enormous magnolia that dominated the front yard of the home, which had been converted to doctors' offices. "This is the building, with the huge magnolia tree that I described to you. This is precisely where I said I'd meet you. That's why I thought you had been here. Odd that we'd arrive at exactly the same time, isn't it?"

"Very odd," said Angela. "Something cosmic?"

"After all these years, maybe," laughed Beth.

Angela turned her attention to the beautiful tree, with the shiny, almost waxy, hunter green leaves. "Whoa, that's a big, old tree!"

"Beautiful, isn't it?" Beth was gazing high up into the spreading branches. "It really sets the building off. This is one of my favorite streets in this old town."

"That," enthused Angela, "is a **major** magnolia. A real land-mark."

"Good meeting place for old friends, and cousins, too," said Beth.

They ate their lunch ravenously, fueled by the desire to play catch up with their respective lives. Laughter ran around their table, spilled from it, settled momentarily, then rejuvenated itself again. Gasping for breath as they sipped their coffee and sweet tea, the cousins reached out for each other's hand as assurance that the day, the hour would not end prematurely.

"You've been here for nine years, now," marveled Angela.

"Yes, and in some ways it feels even longer, because I've been so happy, so comfortable here," mused Beth.

"This was always one of my favorite cities, too," said Angela. "Though I liked living in Louisville, too."

"Well, you've been in Pittsburgh quite a long time. You must feel at home there, by now."

"Not really. I don't know why I've stayed," Angela said, staring at the remains of her Oriental chicken salad. "I got out, I mean I was released and I just stayed. Maybe because of Liz." Her voice choked and trailed to nothing.

"I'm sorry," whispered Beth. "I don't know why I said that. How is your beautiful daughter by the way?"

"How do you know she's beautiful? Though she **is**, incredible as it may seem."

"It's not so incredible," said Beth. "You're beautiful, and Kerry was always a good looking man. You know, the apple never falls far from the tree."

At the mention of her former husband's name, Angela stiffened noticeably. As she gathered about her the careful indifference she always assumed when someone referred to him, she forced a smile and rearranged her bracelets by shaking her wrist.

"I'm glad she lives with him. I'm sure she's a very pleasant young woman when she is with him and his family. With me, she's a real bitch. Understandably, we just do not get along. She'll never forgive me, and there's no reason for her to try to forget."

"How old is she now?" Beth asked, not sure if she should make any more inquiries.

Her cousin was agitated and shaking noticeably. "Seventeen. Trying to be thirty, and acting like a four year old most of the time."

"You don't know that" said Beth, without thinking.

Angela glared at her, and ominously fingered a butter knife. She choked back a shuddering sob, regained some of her composure, and proceeded slowly. "You're right. I don't know that, I seldom see her, and never without him standing guard."

"Well, it's the age, of course," offered Beth. "All daughters and mothers hate each other during the important years, regardless of what went before."

"I don't know. Even if he didn't remind her of the attack, I mean of the incident, of my illness….."Angela's voice again failed her. If I didn't know better, I'd swear she has her period on demand, every time I see her. That's always her excuse when I ask how she's feeling. When I try to offer her something of myself."

Beth tried to lighten the leaden moment. "That's typical. I used that ploy on my mother also."

"I'm serious. When I try to make something surface, she always says she just started. She insists she doesn't hate me, but it's obvious she's scared to death of me.

Angela was talking rapidly, and her voice grew louder and shriller. She was quivering, and the tennis bracelet and its companions were jingling in a less than merry way. Beth was frightened by the palpable rage.

"Perhaps I just wasn't born to be a mother. Perhaps nature or God played a cruel joke," Angela thought, as she attempted to control her shaking by fumbling with and shifting the diamond tennis bracelet, the only gift from her ex that she still retained.

"Are you alright?" inquired her concerned cousin. "Do you want anything else, or should we go?"

"I'm fine," said Angela, unconvincingly. "I don't know why, but I've felt more stress lately. Maybe it's, my daughter, or my entire goddamned past that's always in front of my eyes."

Beth did not want to ask anymore questions about her health, physical or mental. Her cousin, always fragile, seemed like a paper-thin porcelain teacup set at the very edge of a shaky table. Her last stay in the specialized psychological unit of a large clinic in Pennsylvania seemed to have reopened all the buried panic, all the rage and terror that had made her dangerous.

Beth tried to change the subject, but she was unnerved by her cousin's sudden animosity.

"She has always liked Kerry. She was in love with him at one time, probably still is. She'd like to ask about him, but she's scared," thought Angela. She knew the milk of human kindness, of friendship, of love was being curdled in her own heart at that precise moment, and she cared not a whit. Love was turning to hate, for a person she was sure was her last touchstone to reality. She found herself considering her cousin with the same abhorrence that she accorded the young woman in the cab. She began to realize that she could hate her as much as she hated her own daughter.

"You probably have to get back to work. I've kept you long enough," said Angela, briskly.

"I'm in no hurry," answered Beth, though secretly she wanted their meeting to end. Her cousin frightened her, and what had started as a sweet reunion had quickly deteriorated into a frightful confrontation. She wanted to ask about Kerry, but knew better. Let that subject alone!

"Really, I've taken up too much of your valuable time," said Angela, a little too stiffly, a tad too formally to be believable. She had asked for this miserable feeling she told herself. She just had to see her former favorite cousin. Why? To rekindle what? After her last breakdown, to grasp at what? Now, she wanted the afternoon to be over, and she wanted to be gone, to be alone.

"Oh, Gawwd! I sound like Garbo!" She blurted this thought out loud, and was immediately embarrassed.

"I beg your pardon? I don't understand," said Beth. She saw how flustered and confused her cousin was, and felt ashamed for her. She wanted their luncheon and visit to be finished, but she said, "The firm can live without me for a while. I told them it would be a long lunch. Do you want to do something?"

Outside, in the beautiful autumn sunshine, they were frosty with each other. They examined shop windows, glanced at books and sweaters and wines in specialty stores, but there was nothing to say. They drifted toward her hotel, happy that they would soon be saying good bye.

"Maybe you'd like to have dinner tonight?" Beth was not sincere, and Angela saw through the transparency.

"No. Thank you. I just want to turn in early, because I'll be leaving early tomorrow morning."

Sullenly, the afternoon withdrew. As they entered the hotel lobby, lights and soft music made them both a little melancholy.

Beth made another feeble attempt. "It'll be potluck, but you're certainly welcome to have dinner with me. I have a business dinner scheduled, but it's nothing I can't get out of. Someone else could stand in."

Beth tried to sound cheerful, casual, but she prayed that her cousin would refuse the invitation.

"No, really, I want to have a quiet, early night. Thank you, though."

Angela's veracity provided relief for both of them, and they hugged each other tightly. They smiled warmly, as if they were greeting one another.

"Take care of yourself," said Beth, as she clasped her cousin's hand, causing the bracelets to rustle softly. She wanted to comment about the beauty of the tennis bracelet, but restrained herself.

"Yes. You too," said Angela.

"We'll talk, soon. I'll call you," said Beth.

"Okay. Good bye, then."

"Good bye," said Beth, as she moved toward the huge, revolving glass doors.

Angela stood there uncertainly. She waved at her cousin one more time, radiant with relief and delicious depression. Then, as Beth disappeared into the fading autumnal light, she drew a deep breath and walked quickly to the elevators, to retreat to her room to find safety and warmth and quietude.

The Perfect Silver Bullet

It all began with the usual martini discussion with Mr. Curman. Would I try again to make the perfect martini for him? Would I surprise him with a new twist on his old favorite?

It was a beautiful spring evening, with night creeping in carefully, like a burglar cautiously making his way over the surrounding grounds and golf course of the country club. The air had been fragrant with lilac, honeysuckle, and jasmine when I made my way across the rear parking lot, through the employees' entrance, and into the opulent restaurant and dimly lit, spacious lounge.

As I carefully made his double dry, beefeater martini on the rocks, stirring slowly with the big plastic swizzle stick, so as not to bruise the gin, I pointed out what a gorgeous evening we were enjoying. The dapper little man with the neatly tied bow tie turned to his right, to better gaze through the huge picture windows at the far end of the formal dining room. He was seated at his usual spot, near the end of the big shiny bar in the comfortable lounge. That is when I made my move and surreptitiously allowed a single drop of twelve year old scotch to plunk into his martini, stirring all the while, so as not to raise suspicions.

"By jove, Jeeves, I think you've got it!" He was pleased with the first frosty taste.

"Glad you like it, Mr. C. I've been waiting on you, what, three years in this place?"

"Whatever, Jeeves. But, after so many near misses, I think you nailed it with this baby!"

He was too excited over a stinking martini. My name is Gene, but he liked Jeeves, and with what he tipped, he could have called me 'ass wipe' and I'd have smiled and accepted it. I thought him to be a lonely little widower with too much time and money on his hands. I felt sorry for what appeared to be a harmless guy. He had turned the family automobile business over to his son, and was now bored silly. He stopped in the club five out of six nights, and always when he knew I was going to be in the main lounge. Sometimes he ate dinner there, but mostly he just sipped three or four martinis, ate peanuts at the bar, and went home. One night he had more than four. I tried to stop serving him and it was the only time he got lippy with me, so rather than raise a stink in the crowded lounge, I kept serving him watered down martinis. A foxy little number, named Mrs. Mindy Habbert, was seated at the other end of the bar, and was watching me closely, smiling all the while.

When Mr. Curman finally had enough, I talked him out of his car keys and called a taxi for him. When the cab arrived, I walked him through the lounge as discreetly as I could. As I was helping him into the cab he stuck a fifty in my hand. He protested strongly when I tried to give it back, so I resolved to return it to him the next day when I drove his caddy over to his place.

Returning to the lounge, I hustled to refresh the drinks of all my thirsty customers. I was a popular guy because I made their drinks exactly the way they wanted them, kissed up to their rich asses with or without them realizing it, and was the soul of discretion. That last quality is most important, because those rich movers and shakers often want to move and shake with people that are not their primary partners in life. I had seen plenty of marital and commercial cheating in that lap of old money in my three years there, and had been offered pretty decent stipends to keep my mouth shut. I always did.

When it was time to build a new brandy manhattan for Mrs. Habbert, I quietly explained why I had watered Mr. C's martinis.

"I knew what you were doing, lover," she said, as she leaned forward to give me an even better look at her ample breasts. "I think it's sweet how you take care of the idle rich.."

A petite woman, with short dark hair and a ready smile, she was built like a beauty queen, had a husky, whiskey voice, and seemed to enjoy flirting with me. Lord knows I had taken care of her in several precarious situations. As usual, her wimpy, mean little husband had been nowhere in sight that particular evening.

After much prodding, I finally told Mr. Curman the secret of his latest martini.

"You're a clever little beaver, now, aren't you, Jeeves? What did you call it, again?"

"A New York martini, or as they call it around here, a Silver Bullet."

"Well, who'd a thunk it? Not just a triple dry with an olive soaked in vermouth?"

I knew he was playing with me. If he hadn't heard the name of the drink, I was sure he knew the secret of the scotch. We weren't splitting the atom here. So I played along.

"Well, it was pretty dry, but it's still a Silver Bullet."

"How dry, Jeeves?" He was grinning broadly, and popping cocktail peanuts at a rapid rate.

"So dry you should have to blow the dust off it before you can drink it," I said as I left him momentarily to wait on a couple that had just come in.

He was still chuckling when he ordered a refill. "Make it just as perfect as the first one, will you, Jeeves?"

"I'll give it my best shot, Mr. C." I said, then added quickly, "If you'll forgive the puny pun."

The next several times I saw Mr. Curman at the club he was always seated next to Mrs. Habbert at the bar, and they always seemed to have their heads together when I came on duty.

One night he tipped me ten bucks just to check whether the duck looked fresh back in the kitchen. After the chef threw me out and I returned to the lounge, they almost jumped apart at my premature reentry.

The only time they were not together was the rare evening some weeks later when the sawed off, pinch-faced, little Mr. Habbert accompanied his wife. He was twelve years her senior, but looked about 25 years older, and was in a continual foul mood. She was practically bursting out of her lemon yellow spaghetti strapped number, and seemed intent on overtly flirting, damn his presence. Her puffed eyes were overly made up, and a bruise on her cheekbone peeked out from under her face powder. Her husband seemed more interested in which waiter would be serving them dinner in the dining room.

Late that night, just before closing, Mr. Curman and I were alone in the lounge.

"She seems to be quite taken with you, Jeeves."

"Who, Mr. C.?" I bluffed.

"Don't parry, m'boy. Let's talk, frankly," he said, as he leveled an uncharacteristic hard stare at me. "You know, of course, that Mindy is somewhat younger than the estimable Mr. Habbert?"

"I've heard that, yeah." I wondered where this was going.

"She's his second wife, and obviously does not love the little bully, let alone get along with his children, both of whom openly resent her."

He was waiting for a reaction, but I was afraid to register anything. Hell, I was just a working stiff. A thirty-five year old divorced guy, trying to make a living while paying off my ex-wife's bills. I needed the lousy job.

Mr. Curman, always known as the club's best gossip monger, kept at it. "I don't believe he's been much of a companion, let alone lover, for her. She's quite open about her dislike for his very being. You know, she's much closer to you in age."

I was beginning to fidget as I rinsed and reset glasses. It was going to be tough to be discreet in his presence in the future, if he kept filling me in on all his idle gossip. Besides, everything he was saying was widely known around the club anyway.

"I think you two would make a lovely couple, Jeeves." He was laughing again. "I think you two would find that you have much in common."

"Yeah, especially our bank accounts," I said.

He straightened his bow tie and tugged on the cuffs of his elegant, starched white shirt, beneath his equally elegant blue silk suit. "M'boy, don't confuse the situation. With her finances, you'd be set. Besides, she doesn't seem to mind that you're a purveyor of alcoholic beverages. As I said, she seems quite taken with you."

"You trying to broker a deal, Mr. C.?"

He laughed heartily at that suggestion, then grew deadly serious. "She asked me if I thought you would perform an invaluable service for her, and I said you might. Am I correct in that assumption?"

"Depends on what the favor is, Mr. C. I've done favors for her in the past," I answered, cautiously.

"Yes," he said slowly, hesitantly. "She mentioned some of the things you've helped her with in the past couple years."

"What's she want, Mr. C.?"

"Maybe she should address that issue, Jeeves. We'll see." He gave me his brightest smile, laid an extra twenty on the bar, and left.

A week went by and I saw Mr. Curman twice. Both times he smiled conspiratorially at me, stayed for only two drinks, made small talk about golf, and looked as though he was sizing up a job applicant.

The evening after I last saw him, Mindy came in just prior to my closing up the empty joint.

"Am I too late for a scotch and soda?" she asked breathlessly.

She was wide-eyed and nervous, and drank the scotch too rapidly. She leaned forward on the bar, to give me the absolute best view of her unencumbered breasts inside the low cut, silky maroon summer dress. I caught a good shot of nipple as I set the replacement drink in front of her.

After too much rambling about how highly she thought of me, and what a great 'team' we could be, she finished the second drink in a gulp, asked for a refill, and shocked the living hell out of me.

"You want me to what!" I shouted, then looked around frantically, to make sure the place was still deserted. In a whisper, then, "You want me to help you kill your husband? Are you nuts, Mrs. H.? Haven't you heard of divorce?"

"Oh, cut the crap, Gene!" she hissed. "Calling me 'Mrs. H.' makes as much sense as me referring to you as 'my good bartender.' You've taken me home when I was loaded too many times and seen me in various stages of undress, and I've tried every which way I know to get you into bed, so let's not play distant strangers. And that little faggot won't give me a divorce."

"Okay, okay, Mindy," I relented. "But stick to the point. I'm not going to help you kill your husband with some supposed undetectable poison that promises to go to work about four hours after he's taken it. Where'd you ever hear of this stuff and get this cockamamie idea?"

She wanted me to slip it into his after dinner drink after the Country Club's board of directors meeting in the coming month. I always served the board their after dinner drinks by myself, in the board room, and she saw it as the perfect setting to give him the poison, get rid of the vial, and watch him go home to die in his bed overnight. Her research was complete she whined.

After more arguing, shouting, and crying, I placed my hand on her wet cheek, and told her I would help her any way I could, but I was not a murderer.

"I thought you loved me," she sobbed.

She looked like a lonely little girl, in a grown woman's body.

"We've been flirting with lust, Mindy, not love," I said. "But even if true love is developing here, I'm not a killer. Not this type of killer anyway. We're not talking military service." I tried to make her smile, but she smacked my hand away from her face.

"You bastard! You led me on!" She practically spat the words out.

Flabbergasted, I could only sputter, "I led **you** on? Why, why you.....you...."

She stood up and looked at me with such malevolence, I began to feel chills of fear. I had not witnessed that degree of malice in an individual since I irritated my Army drill sergeant.

"If I were you, I'd forget that this conversation ever took place," she threatened in a low, dangerous voice. "This meeting never took place."

Those soft, overstuffed pillows in the front of her dress suddenly looked like loaded bazookas aimed at my heart.

When I came to work the next day, after a sleepless, sultry night, it was so hot and still in the late afternoon, that the parking lot shimmered and the asphalt threatened to buckle. The lot was practically empty but I spotted the block long, dark red caddy.

Mr. Curman was in the men's grill smoking a long aromatic Punch cigar. He said he had just come from the golf course but he sat alone, and his elegant, expensive golf shirt looked perfectly pressed. Also, the only other guys in the grill were playing cards, and looked too fresh to have been on the course on this brutal day. He had never been in the club this early in the years I'd worked there.

When I took my place in the main lounge, he materialized again, taking his usual spot at the empty bar.

"The usual, Mr. C.?" I tried to sound casual.

"Indeed, Jeeves. Your usual perfect silver bullet," he said in his most ingratiating manner.

The small talk ended abruptly when he wondered aloud why I would not want to cash in on a sure thing like the money Mrs. Mindy Habbert would inherit upon the demise of her inadequate and ill suited husband.

"What's in it for you, Mr. C.?" I asked.

"What makes you think I'd get anything for helping a friend, Jeeves?"

"So you **are** brokering this deal. Is the poison your own recipe? Are you her research and development department?" I tried to sound cool and detached, but my heart was pounding like a sledgehammer inside my chest. Instead of flip, I was flattened.

"If I had been you, I would have recognized the opportunity, gone for the gold, and forgotten all about this place, unless you just wanted to work a nothing job," he said without smiling and without any emotion.

I had never seen this side of him. He was an assassin, and he scared hell out of me.

He read my mind when he leveled a frightening gaze, and said, "I had you figured for a bright young man, who would seize the moment, but you didn't. And, for the record, it doesn't matter if I'm the architect of her plan. For that matter, it doesn't make any difference whether I have a role or not. It's none of your business, anymore. You're out of the running. You're out of the money, and you're out of a job. Either that, or you're all out of luck."

He spoke in such a low, monotonous, yet threatening tone, I had to strain to catch it all. But, catch every word and nuance, I did. I was very attentive, and scared shitless. He told me to resign, give my two weeks' notice, and not try to work at another golf or country club in the county, or any neighboring county, as it were.

"I like you, Jeeves," he said with a slight smile. "I always have. Had you figured for street smarts as well as guts galore. You let me down, but I want to take care of you, as best I can. So, resign. Get out. Leave town, okay? Go back to Chicago, you can always get a job there."

He stood up, leaving most of his silver bullet, and stubbed out his expensive churchill. Half of that was left also. He pressed a twenty into my hand with a very firm handshake, which went on a little too long. Looking closely into my eyes, he had my complete attention. With a slight wink, he left the lounge.

My last night at the club was uneventful, quiet, with only a few of my regulars coming in to tell me good bye, good luck, and to tighten me up with a few extra bucks. I had seen neither Mindy nor Mr. Curman in the past two weeks.

The late summer night was muggy and close. A storm threatened in the distance, with rolling, rumbling thunder that was getting louder, as heat lightning flashed a fireworks show in the western sky.

Removing my tie and red bartender's jacket as I walked across the deserted parking lot, I kept a wary eye on the approaching storm. Suddenly, I was bathed in light as a big, dark car screeched around the corner from the front of the building and was bearing down on me.

"Christ," I thought. "Is this how I buy the ranch? Run down in a country club parking lot, with no one to hear my pathetic screams?"

It was Mr. Curman's blood red caddy, and he slammed on the brakes when he reached me.

"Get in, Jeeves," he said in a fairly jovial fashion. "Where you headed?"

"To my car," I said.

"And then?"

"Thought I might go back to Chicago. Kind of miss the old town."

"Wise choice," he said as he stopped at my car.

Before I exited his vehicle, he touched my arm, and then stuck a fifty in my shirt pocket.

"Don't try to return that one, Jeeves, you'll need the money."

"Thanks, Mr. C.," I whispered hoarsely.

"Jeeves, leave soon, okay?" he said as I stood along side his deeply waxed and shined car. Then he motioned me forward and stuck another fifty in my pocket, as I leaned in close to the open passenger side window.

"Soon, Jeeves," he said, giving me an enigmatic yet ominous smile. He looked like a great white shark surveying a solitary, struggling swimmer.

Thursday Ablution

He was staring at the tiles on the floor. They were blood red and pale bronze, and were shaped like checkerboards, with the red ones speckled with ivory, and the bronze flecked with dark brown. The tiles divided the main nave of the church from the wing that contained the confessionals. Penitents shuffled around the corner, from the tiles to the polished wooden floor that led to the left confessional. The one on the right had an equally long line approaching it from the opposite direction. He felt dizzy, as the floor swam before him like a multi-hued brick path.

The young woman ahead of him in line smelled of musk and hair spray, and her bright yellow dress ended above the knee. He had not seen her face, but he knew he wanted to meet her, to talk with her, before the delicious terror would inevitably overtake him. The sound of her two-inch heels on the wooden floor as she walked the eight steps to the confessional box made him focus on her swaying flanks. The rhythm of her heels, crisp yet light, when she exited reminded him of a tiny pony softly trampling the packed clay of its ringed ride for children. Or maybe a quick little flirtatious dance step.

He saw her face clearly; cute, not beautiful; nicely made up, not painted. Her long light brown hair turned up at the ends.

"It's your turn," whispered a voice beside him. A little red-haired girl motioned toward the confessional. He smiled at her and waved her on, ahead of him, so he could spy on the enticing young woman in the yellow dress out of the corner of his eye. It was a mistake he realized when he came out of the box, because the vision was gone from the church. Had he taken his regular turn she might still have been saying her penance, head bowed upon folded hands resting on the pew in front of her. He might have taken the pew behind her, and been able to sniff her perfume and watch her rib cage move ever so slightly with shallow breathing.

Sins he thought; death and sins and sorrow were what he should be concentrating on, as he tried to say his prayers after listening to the priest's lecture. She was nowhere to be found. Should he say his penance quickly and race outside to see which direction she had taken?

It was ridiculous, he was ridiculous. She was attractive, a stranger, maybe a few years older than he; how did he hope to meet her, or even make her notice him? He raised his eyes and glanced across the aisle at the shuffling lines and the hastily retreating reclaimed sinners. He wondered if they smelled of peace, tranquility, absolution, and Friday morning. For him it was still Thursday evening, and a time for contemplation and mumbled prayers. Mumbling went on all around him. Bowed heads, scuffed shoes as they moved in and out of pews and up and down the tiled aisles, and hurried whispers to restless youngsters who were not sure what sins they had committed, all surrounded him. These were his excuses, but the real reason for his inability to concentrate was the delicate object of his daydreams. He whispered his sorrow as he dipped his hand into the holy water and hastily crossed himself. Exiting the church hurriedly, he glanced up and down the main thoroughfare, but no yellow dress was in sight.

It was too hot and dazzling through the rest of the week. He longed for darkness and the coolness of the church. Hot and stifling at his factory job, the air became only a little fresher because of an occasional light breeze through the outfield of the baseball park on Sunday afternoon. He occupied right field, but his mind was still on the girl. Choosing a different mass than the one he usually attended, he searched in vain for her, even dashing to the front steps before the service was ended, so he could carefully view the exiting body of parishioners. The sacred water still rested in beaded form on his forehead.

His hands bled at work. Swinging the heavy lead hammers, knocking out the patterns and wooden frames, stripping the excess corrugated board from the bundles of heavy paper made his arms ache and his blisters crack open and leak plasma mixed with water. Water and wine. The blood of Christ. This is what should have motivated him to attend church on Thursday night, but it was not. The week of sweating and groaning, stripping the paper and fiber board so the residual neat stacks could be turned into beer boxes, and hot dog containers, and potato chip cartons, moved inexorably to Thursday, practice night for the ball club. Again he went to church, to confession, but his confession was to himself. He acknowledged his need to see the girl again, even as he lied to his teammates on his reason for missing yet another practice.

"It's your turn, you know," came the whisper. The old woman smelled musty, her breath of cough medicine.

He waved her on with a vague gesture, and decided it was no good. He had nothing to say in that hallowed box. He knew why he was there, so he occupied a pew in the center of church where he could survey the entire assemblage. An hour later the church was empty and he was sorry he had not arrived much earlier, before the sacrament had begun. If she had been there, she was gone by the time he arrived.

Another mass at a different hour was chosen for the following Sunday, to no avail. She was not at that one either. This ritual of surveying the august gathering, of examining posteriors and faces on the journey to and from the Communion rail, and the inspection of the crowd as it fled the edifice made him feel like a policeman. An officer of the law who was misusing the Lord's edifice and the water in the font.

His most recent missed practice cost him playing time during the afternoon game, and a stern warning not to miss the coming practice on Thursday. He was saved by a savage rainstorm that washed out all outside activity that afternoon and evening, allowing him to get to the church early, a half hour prior to the entrance of the two elderly priests.

They moved slowly to their respective rectangular compartments, composed and somber in their black cossacks and purple stoles, feet faintly scraping the tiles, then the wood. He riveted his attention on each female personage that entered the church. His position afforded him the perfect vantage point for viewing the comings and goings whether emanating from either side door, or the main entrance in back. A wasted evening. She was not there, and he did not avail himself of the grace and peace of the confessional. He told himself he had simply added to his sinful nature, and made the week drag on more slowly. Feeling guilt and remorse on both counts, he left the church without putting his fingers into the holy water.

Another Sunday, another mass time, another long, humid, cruel week. More lies to his teammates and coaches, and skipped beer time with friends. They commented that he did not seem 'right', either on the phone or on the street.

The sticky banality of the other days of the week, the worst of which was Sunday, dripped into a pool of boredom that settled on his soul like hot tar.

Two skipped Thursdays produced spirited, fruitful practices. The pitched batting practice ball looked as big as a Texas grapefruit hung enticingly over the plate on a string. Everyone said he hammered the ball as he had not in weeks. After practice he drank beer with his mates until the bar closed, but it did not block the memory or blunt the feeling. Fear of the opposite sex reasserted itself with suffocating reality at unexpected hours.

The next two weeks were absorbed by overtime in the factory, as much as he could safely handle without falling asleep while driving his automobile. Thus, they were relatively free of frustration and desire. Work, baseball practice and games, beer and forced laughter, and preparation for the coming college term, all combined to form the nucleus, if not the apex of his life during the dog days of that summer. At least they sufficed until another rainy Thursday morning turned into a drowning afternoon and a soggy, waterlogged evening.

The aisle, with its freshly scrubbed tiles, appeared to him like the river Jordan. He felt he would forever stand on its banks. Maybe he would forever stand on the banks of sin. Why was he there that night? What had possessed him to make the trek to repentance, when he was quite positive the journey would end at the river? Crossing the aisle, continuing the toddling migration on the wooden walkway was out of the question tonight. He simply knelt and conversed with a higher order, deep within himself, as securely as his knees sank into the dark red leather kneeler.

Coming from the far confessional he heard the clicking heels, then saw the young, long haired woman cross the aisle and move into a pew in the center nave. He saw her profile, her flipped hair, her dark lipstick, and the tight, short navy dress which had replaced the yellow one.

Breath short and rattling and thudding in his chest, his first instinct was to leave immediately, find his friends, and talk about plans for the coming weekend. He stayed, until she snapped her handbag shut, moved sideways from the pew, genuflected and crossed herself.

Her legs passed the sensuous rhythm to her shoes, and the heels of the shoes to the tiles in the center aisle. His gaze followed her to the back of church and into the main entrance hall, her steady, clipped tapping splitting the sacred silence.

Following her up the street in the muggy, drizzly night air, he felt like a shoddy detective in a cheap mystery novel, trailing his prey. Her swaying hips, in a dress at least one size too small, proved mesmerizing. His unnatural fear of women compelled him to trail her, as if the stalking act would cure him.

Rehearsing his lines of introduction, swallowing his apprehension at appearing half-witted, or worse, he quickened his pace. She walked faster also, without glancing back at him, so he convinced himself she did not hear his footsteps; rather, she was late for an appointment. That surely was the case, as she was fetchingly attired and would certainly be a popular, sought after date or acquaintance. She went to confession regularly, and even though he had been unsuccessful in spotting her at Sunday Mass, she was obviously the type of girl who practiced her religion in serious fashion. Sexy dress and arousing gait notwithstanding, he believed her to be a virtuous person who would be a challenge to meet. Maybe even impossible to approach without the air of an intermediary.

The drizzle had subsided to a sad, gray, grainy curtain, not quite a mist, when she abruptly turned left into a seedy saloon two blocks ahead of him. While she had practically run to her destination, it drew him up short. It was not possible for a woman of her stature, at least in his eyes, to be late for an appointment in that establishment of ill repute. After dawdling outside the shabby bar, surveying the collection of motorcycles parked at the curb, and smelling the tobacco smoke and stale beer every time the front door swung open and closed, he meandered to the next corner, waited for the light, and crossed the street.

Repeating the process on the other side, he finally resolved to enter the bar and search her out. He stood on the curb, opposite the bar, rehearsing once again. Certain changes would have to be made, due to the site of the anticipated meeting, but he felt he was up to the contest, biker bar be damned! Maybe she worked there? No, not dressed like that! Maybe she had just ducked in out of the rain? No, the mist had ended and dissolved into a sodden blanket. Nonetheless, he had to meet her.

Hot, humid, and sweating, he stepped from the curb, then jumped back as a long convertible abruptly swung toward him from the lane of traffic. No signal, no horn, just a rude movement, and he was back on the sidewalk, glaring at the rather greasy looking fellow who jumped from the vehicle and quickly lurched across the street and entered the saloon in question. The driver was oblivious to the young man he had startled and almost hit, as well as to oncoming traffic that had to break suddenly as he strode purposefully in front of it. He had an overall oily appearance, and wore a soiled, preposterous, burnt orange sport jacket, and his hair in a very long greased back style that fell well over his shirt collar.

His appearance matched the incongruous nature of his automobile with its top down on a soggy night like this. The interior of the car glistened with too much drizzle.

The young man had to wait too long for traffic to clear, so he retreated to the corner and caught the light again. By the time he made his way back down the block, the unkempt driver of the moist convertible had emerged from the bar, with his arm around a giggling long-haired girl in a tight navy blue dress that exposed so much leg he wondered if it was ripped.

He froze and watched closely as the happy couple weaved their way through traffic to the vehicle on the other side of the street. An eternity passed before the obviously inebriated driver started the car and recklessly swerved into moving traffic to the delighted squeals of pleasured terror from his passenger. No! It must have been a different girl. One who just looked like her. He felt like an idiot even thinking such a thing.

He looked like a blind man walking past the bar, with his eyes fixed on a distant point. Yet, he seemed to be looking past everything, past his future, past his sins. Why did he suddenly think of sin? Sin and the girl in navy blue, they seemed inseparable.

Suddenly, he stopped. Turning on his heel, he walked hurriedly back to the fetid saloon. It **might** have been a different girl! He entered the bar, just to be sure.

Prettiest Girl in Cincinnati

Her hip-swiveling gait was slowing noticeably, and he wondered if they had walked too far. Worrying about her bad leg, he began cooing to her, telling her how pretty she was, and how proud of her he was, for she had hung in there and walked rather long without complaining.

She looked at him with large, liquid, chocolate eyes. Eyes that could alternate between languid and devilish so quickly it often confused him. Solidly put together, broad and strong, when she stood her ground in a determined mode, legs set wide, she seemed planted, anchored, and ready to withstand gale force winds. Her hair, very short and shiny, was mixed in color tending toward russet. A large head containing an incredible under-bite was set off by amazingly small ears, and gave her a ferocious appearance. She was so homely she was beautiful.

Again he told her she was his pretty baby as they walked down Upper Street in the Gratz Park neighborhood of Lexington. They were sauntering away from Transylvania University that cool, drizzly, foggy night, trying to decide onto which side street to turn to make their way over to Limestone. He reminded her that she would always be his little girl.

He sensed her stiffen, then bristle, before she actually stopped. Then he heard it. A low ominous growl, full of malice and danger. He hoped it was a small dog, but instantly knew it was not. Slowly turning right then left to catch a glimpse of the source of that guttural sound, his skin began to crawl and his neck tingled.

Then it hit him like a sack of wet cement with imbedded shards of glass. It was not a small dog at all. Quite to the contrary, it was large, powerful, with great spring in its legs, and flashing teeth. Its eyes appeared yellow and malevolent, as it coiled, snarled, and began slowly moving toward him again. His right cheek and lower jaw hurt and oozed blood, and both knees felt scraped as he found himself kneeling on the sidewalk. Trying to clear his head, he crawled toward the lawn in front of him when the powerful beast landed again. The dog had broken from a tethered hold and swung a couple feet of chain from its collar as it turned its head and snapped at his face while he tried to protect himself with his arm. He could feel its hot breath as it slashed at him with dangerous fangs and powerful paws. Teeth as sharp as steak knives stuck in his leather sleeve. Instinctively, he rolled up onto the postage stamp-sized, tree-shrouded lawn, trying to shake the foul smelling canine predator. The dog would release its hold, then snap at his face, only to sink its fangs into another part of his leather jacket. He kicked at the beast as he tried his best to protect his face and neck from the furiously snapping jaws. The dog approximated seventy pounds, but its fury was truly the intimidating factor. At one point he tasted his own blood from his left hand as it brushed his mouth after having been ripped by the dog's teeth or nails, or the chain it was swinging from its neck.

Thrashing and rolling, he landed on his stomach and tried to bury his face in the cold, wet ground, and cover his head with his hands. Suddenly the dog was removed from his back. His little girl hit the big dog like John Hunt Morgan, the legendary Thunderbolt of the

Confederacy. She landed with such force that she went over the top of the attacker after tearing it from her master.

She was the most beautifully marked, classically built, female English bulldog he had ever possessed. Calm and patient by nature, she was nonetheless a one-man dog. He and she were all they had in their lives. He had raised her from a seven-week-old pup, and now at about seven years of age, the perfectly marked brindle and white bitch was quite large at better than sixty pounds. Loyalty and devotion to her master was evident, because he was the only human in her daily life.

He was visiting a friend in Lexington for a few days, having driven down from Cincinnati the day before, and since his friend was working late, he decided to take a long walk in the misty, late autumn evening air. It had felt refreshing when they started out, and now it was a hot, sticky, nightmare they were experiencing. The normally gentle, sweet natured bulldog always seemed so passive. She was a gorgeous/ugly, because she was so beautiful inside. On the day his divorce decree became final, his ex-wife, a striking, but cold Northern European blonde, accused him of always loving the dog more than her. He could not and would not deny it. He reminded her he had paid much more for the dog than he had for her! She got the red sports car, he got the bulldog.

Now, this gentle yet powerful bulldog was engaged in mortal combat with a larger, seemingly uncontrollable predator. The ferocity of the fight was shocking. He knew she possessed powerful jaws, as he had witnessed her ability to reduce a golf ball to its liquid core because she needed something to chew as a younger dog, and chewy toys never lasted very long. With her teeth and chunky, heavy front paws she could disassemble and remove the weights from both ends of an old fashioned barbell set of weights. His brother, witnessing this feat once, expressed incredulity. When told it happened with regularity, he opined that maybe she needed an old truck or car battery to play with, that the battery acid might be a little extra treat for her, a pick-me-up as it were. The standing joke in the family was why waste money on milk bones or chew toys when cinder blocks would be appreciated more.

The vicious, snapping, snarling fight moved back and forth across the small, slightly elevated front yard. The two powerful canines were tumbling over each other, their large paws tearing gaping holes in the moist, soft earth. Their large mouths were open and frothing, and their teeth were flashing as they attempted to inflict that last lethal bite. They rolled from under a deep green magnolia tree, tumbling over each other in an effort to gain a position of dominance. The lower branches of the tree quivered and shook, spewing moisture in the air and over the combatants. It made for a curiously luminescent, but horrible sight. He was outraged, panicked, horrified, and proud all at the same time as he scrambled toward them, ineffectually attempting to do something.

They moved away from him, across the lawn and under and around an evergreen bush , which took a terrible beating from the fighting dogs. Viciously and ferociously they attacked one another. It reminded him of a barroom fight he had witnessed when he was in college, with two young men, then four as their companions joined in, throwing beer bottles and swinging pool cues at each other. The men swirled around one another yelling and screaming, swinging fists and beer mugs, and actually gouging and biting in primitive fashion.

These dogs seemed to be attacking each other in the same manner. More than desperate, it was deadly and for a moment, the larger dog had the bulldog on the ground under him. It lunged for her dewlap-covered throat, but she showed remarkable strength and resistance as she shook her head and snapped continuously. She rolled toward the evergreen, with the larger dog still trying to maintain its position of strength on top of her. She gained leverage as the predator was knocked into a stiff lower branch and quickly the bulldog was on top of the aggressor, with a death grip on its neck. The other dog started to scramble from under the shrub, but after maneuvering about three feet the bulldog tightened its grip on the side of its neck, and the struggling began to wane.

He cautiously approached them and grasped his little girl's harness by its top strap. He could hear her breathing hard, and she appeared to be snorting moisture as well as air through her pug nose. The only thing that kept the other dog alive was the fact that the bulldog's death grip was over a large leather collar as well as neck muscle. She was not about to let up, no matter how soothingly he talked to her. Assuring her it was okay, and that she could let go he began to tug gently on her harness. No, she would not let go, and continued to shudder as her breath rushed harshly through her nose. He had seen her in this mode before, when she got her jaws on something she desperately wanted. Whether a kid's soccer ball or an old scarf someone discarded, if she had it, she kept it.

Then, the other dog made a quick move to regain its stance, and it was enough to loosen the bulldog's grip. He jumped back from them, sure that the battle would rage again. As he slipped and fell to his hands and knees on the wet turf, he heard a resounding clang, and the larger dog yelped in agony and ran from the yard, across the street and down the block. It ran with a noticeable limp, shrilly yelping in pain the entire way. He reached for his bulldog as she instinctively started in pursuit of the attacker. Her natural reaction was short lived, as he barely had to put his hands on her broad formidable front shoulders and she collapsed, panting heavily, and laid on her side. Her tongue was hanging out of the side of her bloody mouth.

"That's a helluva dog you got there." The voice was soft, contralto, near south, and comforting. It was the second time he had heard that description of his bulldog.

A couple years earlier they had been walking on a beautiful Sunday afternoon through the schoolyard of a junior high school. Rounding a corner of the spacious main building, he noticed a soccer tournament in progress at the adjacent athletic field, and they stopped to watch some of the action. Keeping one hand on her leash and the other on the top strap of her heavy-duty harness, he watched her as closely as she did the action on the field. He knew what she wanted; just let that ball get a little closer and it would be hers, for life. The large black man had a kid playing in the tournament, but he was more interested in the bulldog. Apparently, he cared little for his wife's dog, which he described as a 'small yapper', and craved a larger, more powerful pet. He asked many questions about the bulldog, in particular, and the breed in general. Ignoring his kid's team on the field, he continually stroked the dog's head, patted her side and mentioned how sturdy she was. He said how much he would rather have a dog like that than the silly little thing his wife had at home. The bulldog loved the attention, and glanced back and forth between master and admirer. It was as if she knew she was on display, and as the black parent walked away he looked back admiringly and mentioned for the fourth time, "That's a helluva dog you got there."

Cognizant of outdoor lights being lit on some of the surrounding houses, he found it odd that the house with the torn up yard and bushes was dark. A figure stood over him holding a long handled garden spade with a small shiny head. The soft woman's voice spoke again. "Are you alright?"

Before he could answer, she said, "Is your dog okay?"

The bulldog was still panting, but not as heavily as previously, and he stroked her soft little ears, her smooth side, and her silky wrinkled head. She was looking up at him as he whispered to her that she was going to be all right, that he was proud of her, and that he would take care of her.

"Why don't you bring her in the house?" The woman squatted down, still holding the spade that she used to whack the predator's ribs. She looked over both of them carefully.

He gently held the dog in his arms as he struggled to get to his feet. She was heavy, and though she did not wriggle very much, she whimpered and felt like dead weight. With the aid of the spade-wielding avenging angel, he secured his dog in his arms, and limped to her house next door. Porch lights were going out as he glanced back at the battleground.

"Don't worry, they're outta town. Boy, will they be surprised when they get home." She had read his mind.

Her kitchen was warm and homey, cluttered and old and full of bric-a-brac. It smelled great, like she had just baked cookies or a pie. He felt safe, and tears began to well in his eyes as that feeling of being in a safe harbor mixed with the sorrow he felt as he looked down at his battered bulldog laying on a throw rug on the kitchen floor. She suddenly seemed smaller, weaker, more vulnerable than she ever had in the time he owned her.

He barely had time to ask for a wet rag, when his hostess was handing him two warm, wet, soft washcloths. One he used on the dog, relieved to see much of the dried blood coming off easily, and exhibiting few wounds beneath it, meaning that much of the blood belonged to the vanquished attacker. The other cloth he used on his own face, ears, neck and hands. He was a bit chewed up, but nothing felt out of place, and his hostess was not staring at him as if he were the hunchback of Notre Dame.

Again she read his mind. "You'll both survive. You don't look too worse for the wear. No scars for either of you. Shame I don't have medals for you both."

His jacket had taken a beating, but had saved him from serious injury. His pants were ripped and muddy, and his sneakers were a mess. Other than that, and the fact that he was full of the predator's stench, his appearance was not too bad, as he surveyed himself in the mirror over the kitchen sink. His face was scratched and cut, as were his neck and hands. Hydrogen peroxide was cleaning up man and dog alike, and his guardian angel appeared to be enjoying the role of Florence Nightingale. She helped him gently clean up the dog, and put a bowl of water down for her to drink. Then she put a few plain shortbread cookies on a small mat for the dog to nose around before she gingerly started eating them.

She was a plus-sized, but certainly not fat, youngish woman of indeterminate age. She appeared to be strangely old fashioned, and quietly hip at the same time. Her very straight long dark hair was beginning to be streaked with silver and was worn parted in the middle. She continually tucked her hair back behind her ears, revealing them to be smallish but slightly protuberant. Notwithstanding, they were attractive, pierced, and set off by lovely sapphire earrings. Her face was wide, with a small mouth, full lips, and large, kind gray-blue eyes.

She did not talk in the rapid fire, staccato fashion of the Bluegrass Region. Some people in that area speak as if they are double-parked. Instead, she was calm, funny and deliberate and when he wondered aloud whether the attacking dog might have been rabid, she snorted, "No, not rabid, just mean. I know for a fact he attacked a neighborhood kid last week, just up the street. The cops came. That damn dog has been tested too many times, 'cause he's always after someone. He even bit someone walkin' up their front steps. He's not rabid, just a damn nuisance. The cops ought to take him away, or the critter control ought to put him down. They just make 'em use a stronger rope or chain, and he keeps breakin' loose."

She hesitated, and staring at the relaxed bulldog on her kitchen floor said, "I'm glad you and your dog kicked the shit out of him. Maybe he'll stop now. Or, maybe he'll just keep runnin' 'til he gets hit by a truck or somethin'."

She said it so quietly and wistfully it did not sound like swearing. It did not even sound mean. He thanked her again, and told her he was glad she was there with the shovel, and that she handled it like Annie Oakley with a rifle.

She laughed and said, "Wouldn't have missed it for four tickets to a 'Cats game against L.S.U. Besides, I wouldn't have had the guts to hit the bastard if your pooch hadn't pinned him down in the first place."

Once again he marveled at the tone of her voice. It was full of mirth, yet calm and soft. Nothing vindictive there, despite the vulgarity and earnestness of the sentiment.

They talked at the kitchen table, as he slowly windmilled his right arm and probed his right shoulder with his lightly bleeding left hand. Sore and worn out, he sipped her delicious, strong coffee and reached for another cookie. He was more interested in what she had to say than he was in his physical condition, and admired the way she moved about the comfortable room with an easy grace.

Her name was Alice, which seemed absolutely perfect for her; an old fashioned name, sturdy, solid, yet sweet and gentle. She had moved to Lexington five years earlier to get married. Instead, she was jilted, but stayed because she fell in love with the city. He guessed she was not from the area, because her voice was so calm and deliberate. Again, the laugh, and she asked him to guess where she was from. He said somewhere around Louisville; no, south and west of there; no, maybe across the river in southern Indiana.

"Damn! You're good," she stated. "I'm from right outside Evansville."

Now it was his turn to laugh. She asked where his friend in town lived. How much farther did he and the dog have to go? When told they were walking back toward Dudley Square, she protested. "That's too far! I don't want you two walking anymore. I'll drive you back."

Her proprietary statement made him feel warm and expansive. He liked the sound of urgency in her voice. He protested however, and asked if he could use her phone to call his friend since it would not be advisable to force the dog to walk anymore that night. His hostess put her hand on his injured left hand and said softly, " I'd really like to give a lift to you two heroes."

Again, gratitude and affection welled up inside him, and he nodded his head as he slipped from his chair and knelt on the floor by his dog. She was laying on her side now, and began to wag her stumpy little tail as her master began whispering to her and stroking her head. He was wiping more dried blood from her neck and throat as he closely inspected her for more serious injuries. She began to lick his injured left hand, and to Alice it almost appeared that the bulldog was trying to clean blood from him just as he was doing the same for her.

"What's her name?" asked Alice.

"Tootsie," he responded. "Her name is Tootsie."

"That's a cute name. Why'd you call her that?"

"When I first took her home, she was a very young small pup, and she was pushing a kid's big plastic kickball all around the kitchen and dining room. She'd hit it with her little pug nose and then chase after it. I called to her several times, trying out different names, to see how they sounded. 'Daisy,' 'Brandy,' you know, several kinds of dog names. She didn't respond to any of them. Just kept chasing that big ball back and forth. Until I called 'Tootsie'! Then she stopped for a second and looked at me, before she went back to chasing that ball. So, I named her Tootsie. Not very aristocratic for a bulldog that has paperwork behind her name from here to Knoxville and back, huh?"

"I think it's perfect."

He looked down at his dog. The glint had returned to her eyes, and she continued to wag that corkscrew little tail. He realized she was responding to his mention of her name.

He leaned down and whispered into her ear again. Her tail moved faster and she rolled to an upright position.

"What did you say to her?" asked Alice.

"What I always tell her. That she's the prettiest girl in Cincinnati."

Alice stared down at them from her seat at the kitchen table. "Bravest girl in Lexington as well. That's a helluva dog you got there."

Then, after a long pause and a deep sigh she added, "I'll get the car."

A Hero's Welcome

Mehringer came home from the service exactly two years from the date he had left. He returned to the small, steely, smoky Pennsylvania city in 1970, in nondescript clothes, carrying his duffel bag and too many memories. At first, he felt the need to talk about his experiences but no one wanted to listen. Later, when people asked questions, he could not bring himself to talk about the Army or his unique perceptions, though bitterness toward involvement in the war was steadily growing in his mind.

As the winter wore on, grindingly and depressingly oppressive, he developed a distaste for everything civilian. He found himself lying to friends who had not had to report for military service in order to communicate with them in any capacity. His naps on the living room sofa grew longer even though he slept later into the morning hours. He felt safe curled into the fetal position, knees hugged into his chest. His initial attempts at employment were blunted by his own honesty during the interviews. Being brutally frank about his aspirations in light of perceived deficiencies in the prospective employer offered small chance at employment, his educational accomplishments notwithstanding. His cousin, Artie, a former Marine who had been out of the service for six years told him he had to shake off this lethargy and rejoin the civilian population. He told him he had gone through the same malaise, that he had felt out of touch and unwanted when he returned after three years in the Corps, but he had forced himself to find work. Then he returned to night school, and got married.

Mehringer told Artie he did not feel unloved, just misunderstood. He felt it impossible to describe how much he missed some of his Army buddies, how routine civilian life felt, how he wanted to avoid responsibility and consequential actions. And, he certainly was not looking for a girl, and most assuredly wanted nothing to do with marriage. He accused Artie of talking to him on behalf of his mother. His mother loved him too much to confront him with her fears, so she enlisted his cousin to broach the subject. Artie protested. He said it was strictly his idea, that he hated to see him wasting time and becoming locked into his Army remembrances.

"They're dangerous, Teddy," said his cousin ominously. "Take it from me, you can get yourself all knotted up inside. You remember how easy it was in the military, giving orders, taking orders, no thinking. Now, you gotta make decisions, make a new life for yourself, and you think no one cares."

"Oh, they might care," Mehringer said. "I just don't think anyone understands, and when you start to relate, when you try to explain, they look at you like you have lobsters coming out of your nose. Eventually, their attention wanders."

"So, why don't you contact a couple of your buddies? Guys who got out around the same time as you. See how they're doing. Might make you feel better."

"Do you think that's wise?" Mehringer doubted the integrity of his cousin's suggestion, and he studied his face closely.

"No," answered Artie, truthfully. "It'll probably send you back into a 'blue funk', but it's better than constantly screwing yourself up in job interviews. Either that or go back to grad school. Or, find a girl and get married."

They both laughed heartily at that, and went downtown to drink beer and shoot pool.

One morning his mother woke him earlier than usual and asked him to have breakfast with her before she left for work at the five and dime store. They sat, and talked long after they had finished their ham, eggs, and goetta. He wondered if she was going in at all, she would be so late.

She waved the question away dismissively. "They get plenty of hours out of me. I go in early most of the time, and I haven't had a Saturday off in so long, they owe me a little time with my son."

He got up to refill his coffee cup, knowing what was coming and dreading it.

"Ted, don't you think you should do something about your future?" Her voice was calm, but he could hear the worry.

"I'm doing something about it, ma," he responded. "I'm getting older and wiser with each passing day."

"That's not funny. You need to do something. All you do now is run around with your cousin, keeping late hours, drinking." She hesitated, then added, "And he should be home with his wife."

"I don't know, ma. Nothing seems right to me. Nothing in the way of a job sounds right. I've been thinking of reapplying to grad school."

"Do you have money for that?"

"No, I'm running out of money. My Army dough is gone and I've dipped into my savings. I thought maybe the G. I. Bill would pick up a pretty good chunk of it."

"I'd rather see you get a job, and go to school part-time. Wouldn't that make more sense?"

He ignored the question and began to glance at the morning newspaper. After a long sigh, his mother gathered up the dishes and put them in the sink, and kissed the top of his head. She asked him to think about talking with one of the managers at the large downtown bank where he had worked prior to his entry into the infantry.

When he mentioned this to Artie that evening his cousin said he thought it was a sound idea. "Weren't they paying for your grad school?"

"Only a small part of it. I really don't want to go back there. I don't want to be a banker."

"I know," said Artie. "Everything looked so damned dull to me when I first got out."

"Nothing around here has changed," Mehringer said. "And everything about me feels different. I'm not the same guy I was. I can't explain it."

"You don't have to explain anything to me," said his cousin. "But you gotta snap out of it. Let's get a beer."

He borrowed money from Artie to put gas in the Ford, and they followed 112 down the hill where it became one of the main streets in the heart of the city. He eased past the Court House and the new civic arena and crossed the river to the iron producing twin city on the east side of the river. He cut left on Fourth Street and through a tough neighborhood of old factories, railroad yards, dirty saloons and tattoo parlors. When Artie asked where he was headed he said he did not know, he just thought they should head out of town, at least away from their side of the metro area.

They passed cut-rate variety stores, a boarded up department store, and some discount furniture emporiums before the area

138

became mixed with low-income residential property. He turned right onto a main drag that climbed steadily toward the airport. Fast food restaurants, liquor stores, and bars and grilles dotted both sides of the highway. He abruptly pulled into a parking lot. The lighted signs promised billiards, beer and burgers. Inside it was dark and dank. They drank beer, watched a basketball game on the television over the bar, and Artie flirted with an inebriated dark haired woman with large breasts who insisted she was not wearing any underpants.

He told Artie on the way home that he did not think he would ever get married. He did not even want a woman in his life. Well, he did, but only on his terms. He did not want to become bored with someone and then have to go to the trouble of trying to replace them in his life. Artie asked him if that is what he thought he was doing.

Mehringer glanced at him and smiled as he stopped at a bar closer to their residential area. At his cousin's urging, he again said he might call some of his old Army buddies.

O'Mara, in Boston, said he was doing fine. He was working for his brother-in-law in a real estate office, learning the business and studying for his examination. He told Mehringer he would be down to visit him sometime over the summer, when things settled down a little. Better still, he thought Mehringer should come stay with him for awhile, get a fresh view of life, see if New England looked promising. When Mehringer asked him if he was having trouble readjusting to civilian life the answer was swift. No, he rested a couple weeks, then went right to work with his brother-in-law. He received a great welcome home, and life was proceeding swimmingly. He asked about his friend's reception when he arrived home in Pennsylvania.

"Great," said Mehringer. "Just super."

Morales, in Bridgeport, was having a difficult time. He had received a hero's welcome and his younger sisters were awed by his medals. His mother treated him like a king for the first few weeks, making his favorite breakfasts and dinners, and not bothering him to talk about his war experiences. His uncle did not push too hard, but had asked some questions that were uncomfortable and made him lie. He could not tell any of them about the court martial, even though he beat the rap, but his uncle could not understand why he ETS'd as only a corporal, when he had seen so much action and had all the medals and citations. He asked Mehringer if he was sleeping and had any money left. Morales was broke, had no car and no way to get to Pennsylvania, and could not remember the last time he had slept uninterrupted through the night. He said he would love to see his friend, and asked if Mehringer wanted to come to Bridgeport. They could hang out and it would be an excuse for both of them to keep from looking for jobs until they had their minds right. He asked what his reception had been like in Pennsylvania.

"Like yours, a hero's welcome," he lied. "Hail the conquering hero."

Two nights later he and Artie were at a tavern near a fire station where a guy who played softball with Artie worked. They were talking about the coming season and attempting to get him to join the team. He resisted because baseball was still in his blood and he thought he might contact the team he played on before he left for the Army. His cousin then brought up the subject of job hunting again after he told them of his recent phone conversations with his Army pals. He reiterated that he did not want to return to the bank, that he had no interest in the banking trade.

"Not all banks are the same," said the fireman. "Not all training positions are the same. Maybe you should look into what another bank has to offer. Seems to me most of them are always looking for help."

"Yeah," chimed in Artie. "Maybe you just have a bad taste because of your experience with that big bank downtown. You could talk with one of the newer suburban banks. They might have something you'd be interested in."

"I don't want to be a banker, in any capacity. I'm not interested in exploring other opportunities in the banking trade," he said, with

140

what he felt was finality. "Besides, all those suburban banks are just branches of the big banks downtown, on either side of the river."

"Well, I could put you in touch with the branch manager at my bank," offered the fireman. "He's a nice young guy, real smart, but easy to talk to."

"I don't want to be a banker," Mehringer said quietly.

"He goes to my church. I see him all the time." The fireman was persistent. "Why don't I mention your name to him. You know, give him your background and your phone number. It couldn't hurt."

"I don't want to be a banker, I don't think I'd have any aptitude for it."

"Yeah," said Artie to the fireman. "Mention his name to your banker. If you stop in to see him, why not pick up an employment app for Teddy. Then, when he fills it out, he could call your friend, and make arrangements to drop it off."

"Okay, I'll do it," enthused the fireman. "I'll get in there day after tomorrow and get the app. I'm sure he'll be interested in talking to him."

They were talking about him, around him as if he were a stick of furniture. The beer was taking the edge off. He did not care. He did not want to feel complicated, he wanted a smooth, even life, and this was getting complex.

"You'll fill out the app, won't you Teddy?" Artie had suddenly brought him back into the conversation. "You'll talk to the banker?"

He slowly nodded, and took another long drink of beer. He would not fill out the application. He would not see the banker. His life would not be made complicated by a bunch of strangers. He did not want to lead a life like theirs, but he could not tell them that, so he just drank and nodded. Tomorrow he would borrow some money from his mother and drive to Bridgeport to see Morales.

Coffee Sense

Okay, let's get this straight, right from the start: I'm not a fool, I've never been considered a foolish person, thus, I don't suffer fools easily.

My ex has acted foolish; no, he has acted like a moron from time to time, and worse yet, the imperfections of his various actions appeared designed to make me feel and look ridiculous. That's why I decided not to take him back. Well, I decided that after having coffee with my good friend, Luz. She is decidedly one of the smartest, sanest, most perceptive people I have ever known. Besides being imbued with great common sense, she is patient. She listens closely, makes a point or ventures an opinion only upon request and then bides her time until her valuable advice invariably finds its mark. If it is not accepted, or questioned needlessly, she simply shrugs and wishes you well. Her life seems to be ordered, and if yours isn't, well, she can offer only so much help. She insists that street smarts cannot be found in blind alleys.

She listened to my rants against my ex-husband many years ago, and offered estimable guidance, which helped me to keep my head glued on straight. My ex-husband is not to be confused with my current ex, who is a man that has flown in and out of my life with all the distraction of a black fly buzzing about my head and face, but whom I never married. I came close once, but didn't thank God, because he can really become an insufferable bastard. He has been a constant in my life, thus, he's my ex. A constant what? Constant presence, yes; constant surprise, maybe; constant source of irritation, definitely.

When I stopped seeing him the last time I felt it had to be permanent. I experienced the usual feared let down, but it was a kind of relief as well. I mean, it wasn't as though there was another adventure to begin. There was no other man, no other lover around the next corner, or hidden away in my life and just waiting to be retrieved. Not that I couldn't attract another guy. I know there're more of us than them, but I'm a reasonably attractive woman, with a pretty firm figure for someone rapidly approaching fifty. I've got all my teeth, a nice smile, no phony color in my hair, and I'm told I look good in shorts and a halter top.

Okay, okay, I know those are all just physical attributes, and not lasting qualities. But, I said "attract" not "meet" or "engage". I'll admit I can be a bitch, very critical, quite impatient, and too demanding, but I'm generally loyal, unless the party to whom I've been faithful treats me like a pile of dog crap out in the middle of a cantaloupe patch. And, that's what my ex did. He admitted he still thought about his former girlfriend, and when I pressed him further on the subject, he told me she calls him every so often. How rude, to say the least. I mean him, not her! He didn't have to tell me that, no matter how much I pried. A gentleman, at least an intuitive one, would have allowed me to rant and rave, and then would have assured me nothing was going on between them, and no contact was ever made. Furthermore, he could have said he told her to piss off, or he could have made up some stupid story about a song he just heard, or a movie on television he had seen recently that reminded him of her. I wouldn't have bought it, but it, but it would have allowed me to save a little dignity. But, not my ex. No, he's so damned honest! You know how the honest ones can be? Big, wide eyes, little boy look, all full of hurt and presumed innocence? Then, when you least expect it, they drop a big bomb on you. That's how he handled it, the asshole!

I'm getting myself worked up, and I shouldn't, because he's out of my life now, and he's not getting back in.

The drama should have played itself out when he came over to get some clothes and other items that he had stored at my place. There were also mementos to be cried over in common. I did not weaken, however, even through the occasional passionate, unconsummated embraces, though I did find him truly vulnerable at that time, and even endearing. The obligatory final, parting kiss lasted a little too long and was a little too open-mouthed and probing, but that was my fault as much as his. I guess the terror of being alone again was not totally exorcised, and suddenly I found myself wondering what I would do. I mean, it's not like I haven't lived alone, and loved it. In fact, I really prefer my own place, alone and comfortable and lived in. However, the solitary evenings at home with a good book, or an old tearjerker on television, or the decision to not go to bed at all, and just doze on the couch between too many sips of wine were always my choice, on my time. When I wanted him around, or when he asked me to stay over at his place, it was an arrangement that we both welcomed and could make sense of, and we were certain to share our joy in measured statements, less the process appear too natural and inevitable. Thank God neither of us said something stupid like wanting to "remain friends". I may have been nervous about the coming changes in my life, but I certainly did not want to pretend to be something I wasn't, or anything I had no intention of becoming.

At any rate, these past months have limped by, harmlessly as well as aimlessly. I've socialized with a few of my girlfriends, and I've entertained. I even had a dinner party, which went pretty well considering it was all couples, plus me, the solo falsely happy hostess. At least I did not have to pretend that I had another engagement, and leave early. So, if things have not gone swimmingly, at least they have gone, and the ignominy of arriving alone at social gatherings and then lying my way out early, trying to look as if I had somewhere to go, has

145

left me resigned to my fate. At least I'm coping with what appears to be my destiny, until I'm finally over him.

Don't misunderstand, please, I know I'm over him, it's just that sometimes I've felt that I burned a bridge behind me. Maybe I should have had another man in my life before I cut all ties with the last one. I don't know what I saw in him, although he is cute, in a primitive sort of way. He's not as intelligent or well educated as I am, though that was never too important, but he isn't even street smart. And that did bother me; I told you I don't tolerate foolish people. I mean, how do you explain for example, getting rid of a perfectly good, late model sedan, which has given you no trouble, and buying a brand new pick-up truck that you cannot afford, when you just lost your job? The only person more stupid was the jerk who loaned him the money!

Well, the only reason I'm still wrestling with this entire question, even though I know I'm better off without him, is because he called recently. He sounded forlorn on the telephone. He sounded miserable, lonely, and stupid, but a bit like a lost little boy also. He wants to see me, says he misses me, and hasn't talked with his old girlfriend for a long time. He said she's engaged to some car salesman. Hah! Can you believe I'd fall for something like that? Like I even give a good Goddamn! I told him off, then thought about him non-stop for 48 hours, until he called again. As I said, he's cute, in a Cro-Magnon fashion, and all his parts were in the right spots, and in good working order, the last time I had occasion to check. However, I just have this feeling he is always going to be a decidedly bad risk.

When he called a third time I agreed to meet him sometime after work, for a drink. I'm not taking him back, though. I told him that, and he grew silent. I said I'd call him to set it up, and I clearly could hear his deep sigh. It made me go all soft and dreamy, but only for an instant. We couldn't possibly make it work. No, I'm better off with him out of my life, even if I can't sleep, and I'm worthless at my job. At least I have a job. I'd have to support the worthless creep. No, he's not getting into my life again.

However, I suppose it would be rude not to call him. On the other hand, it would be absolutely vulgar to meet him for the purpose of one last roll in the hay. There must be some middle course, but I'm not sure I can fathom what or where it is. I don't think I'm strong enough to just talk with him over a scotch and soda. And, I damn sure know he isn't!

It would probably be best if I just called him and discussed things over the phone, without agreeing to see him. Then, if he insisted on a meeting, I would have stated my case clearly and logically, and our encounter would be strictly platonic. Well, it would be a meeting with ground rules, anyway. I think that is what I'll do. Even though he is not getting back into my life, I'll call him. But, I think I'll call Luz first, for coffee.

Spotty Morgan

I can see my old street as clearly right now as if I lived there just yesterday. It is as precise in my memory as what I was doing and where I was when I heard the news about Kennedy having been shot. Over fifty years later, and the houses and their occupants loom as large as the black numbers peering through the crystal on my aunt's dining room clock.

She lived across the street from us and had a dog, Jigsy. Jigsy was famous in the neighborhood for stealing things, and hiding them in the basement or in my aunt's shed in her backyard. Jigsy really liked to heist things that he could easily carry, and did not have to struggle to drag home. Whenever a kid could not find a prized baseball, tennis ball, doll, or catcher's mitt, they proceeded to my aunt's house where she would invariably find the object only carelessly hidden. Jigsy did not mind returning objects so long as he was not prevented from stealing them again.

Dogs formed a focal point for the kids on our street. You identified certain people and their homes by the pet they had. Mr. Loomis had a fat little pug. They had the same gait, the same pushed in, scrunched up appearance. Mr. Loomis may have lived three houses from the end of the block, in the brown house with the droopy yellow shutters, but that is not what identified him, or his residence. No, he was the guy who owned the pug. Just as my aunt owned the thief, and the elegant black people, the Jacksons, at the other end of the block, where it crossed Cedar Avenue, had the small, sleek dog that loved to jump in and out of their beautiful dark blue Buick. Cats did not count for much on my street. A couple neighbors owned cats, but they were kept inside most of the time, and did not seem to have personalities. The dogs all had their own identities. Oh, the Bartholomews had a big, regal looking white cat that protected his turf pretty well, but he liked to slink around in a sneaky fashion too much to please us kids. You could not get close to him, because he was capable of ripping several layers of epidermis from you with one swipe of his large paw. Their house was larger than the others on the block, and set back farther from the street than everyone else's. Alexander looked bored and mean, perched on a fence at the end of their long driveway. No, cats didn't count!

Our dog, Tippy, was supposed to be a wirehaired terrier. He was a "Heinz 57", or as my dad referred to him, a "mixed purebred". He was black and white and gray, and had a head like a terrier's, and fluffy, if not wiry fur about his chest and shoulders. The rest of him was too convoluted to describe, except for the smooth coat from mid-section to tail. When my dad brought him home to surprise my mother with the fox terrier she had always wanted, he got a response he did not expect. She simply inquired, "What is <u>that</u>?"

While he was not repulsive looking, Tippy sure was not going to be chosen as a stand in for Rin Tin Tin. No one in the family readied a speech for acceptance of "best in show", either. His true virtue was his loyalty, which can only be described as fierce. Sometimes he was a little too fierce, and became confused when play among kids got out of hand. He had the run of the neighborhood, as did most of the dogs on the street, and always seemed to be in the thick of the action, whether it was stickball under the street lamps at night, backyard football, or building roads in someone's sandbox. As such, he watched closely when my brothers or I were involved in the game, and if it appeared we were getting hurt, he would jump in and grab some poor kid's sleeve or pant leg, until we firmly convinced him it was just a game and we were okay. If he did not care for an adult, it was a different story, and all bets were off.

My uncle, who had just moved out of our house and into a place of his own, still joined us for dinner at least three or four times per week. He remained a part of the immediate family, and enjoyed watching the kids in the neighborhood play, grow, mature. He witnessed Tippy grow from a pup to a loyal young dog who protected his nephews, and this pleased him immensely. He pinned the monicker "Pants Tearer, Baby Scarer" on Tippy, because when in doubt, the dog gave no quarter, and had ripped several adults' trousers who were in proximity to us kids when games grew rambunctious. There was no rhyme or reason to the action by the dog; he knew he couldn't chomp down on a youngster, but an adult that was handy was another matter. His bark, loud and shrill, was the cause for the second half of the nickname. Even a greeting to a family member was sudden and explosive, and it caused many small children on our street to awaken abruptly from naps, or bolt upright in their walkers, and begin bawling loudly.

Not everyone on our block was as enamored of our dog as were we. We found that out the hard way. Kids loved Tippy, because as time went by he became as protective of those he saw regularly as he did family members. At least he protected the children that we played with most of the time. If an interloper to our block, a tough kid who was there to pick a fight, got too smart with one of our friends, a simple "Sic 'em, Tip" was enough to send the miscreant on their way. Some adults in the neighborhood, however, did not seem to appreciate the dog's expressions of fidelity.

Then there were the Morgans, who lived in a brick, one story house on the other side of the street from us, and about seven houses away. They were generally nice, quiet middle-aged people, with grown children, and one of their fathers' at home with them, who everyone in the neighborhood referred to as "Grandpa". He was hard of hearing. No! He was a stone deaf skinny little guy who wore a useless hearing aid that had wires hanging out of it, and was connected to nothing. They just flopped there all the time, against the front of his cruddy flannel shirt that he wore summer and winter. It was always buttoned up, even at the cuffs and neck, and even on the hottest summer day, and it can get pretty stinking hot and humid in near-south river cities.

He wore a dirty, checked cap that vaguely resembled a snapped front golf hat, and greasy, baggy pants held up by a leather belt capable of wrapping around his tiny waist at least twice. Grandpa may not have been able to hear even if he had connected the hearing aid, because he only had one ear. The missing ear was replaced by a gnarled stump that protruded from the side of his head, but wasn't capable of holding his hat straight, or supporting eyeglasses. When he sat on the front porch on hot summer afternoons, training his binoculars on passing high school girls dressed in shorts and sheer cotton blouses, he gave the appearance of someone who had a perpetual question on their mind, or had their head cocked at an odd angle so as to better hear the conversation.

Grandpa had a dog, too. His name was Spot, and he was short and lean, just like Grandpa. His short mostly white coat contained several large black blotches, thus his name. Though, in retrospect, I believe he should have been named "Blotch" or "Blemish" instead of Spot. The dog was an extension of Grandpa. They began to resemble each other, and grew dirtier together through the years, though Spot did have two good ears. Grandpa didn't like the kids on the street and neither did Spot. He was identified so closely with his master that kids began referring to him as "Spotty Morgan", the same way they would call a pal or friend or acquaintance on the street by their entire name: Tommy O'Neill, Judy Zimmer, Frannie Blochner, and Spotty Morgan.

Spotty was not a problem during the winter, when he spent most of his time in or near his master's house. It was during the rest of the year that he became a nuisance to the children on the street. Like kids in residential sections of old cities everywhere, we preferred playing in the streets and alleys close to our homes as opposed to hiking numerous blocks to a playground that might already be crowded. Games were spontaneous and traffic was lighter in those wondrous years immediately before and during the Korean War, especially at night.

Night in the dead of winter could be mild and foggy, but even when it was unusually cold, it posed no threat to ingenuity. Games could be imagined quickly, and teams chosen rapidly. The crunch of packed snow under foot on a clear, starlit, calm night lent an air of mystery to the scene. Buildings, trees, light poles, all appeared surreal to the kids as they hollered back and forth, chasing each other or an elusive kick ball, breath being puffed forth like spun glass. At night, games in outside winter weather took on a prismatic quality.

Summer, ah, that was magical, however. The long, hot, humid days gave way to sticky fun filled nights under the streetlights. Kids dashed down narrow driveways to the sidewalk, and back and forth across small front lawns, to porches where adults sat and talked in hushed tones. They casually observed sweating boys playing stickball in the street, stopping the game momentarily as the occasional automobile crept down the street. Fireflies lighting up the lawns and neat gardens were matched in intensity by glowing tips of cigarettes and cigars on front porches, as fathers, uncles, and older cousins discussed the Truman administration, or Ike's campaign, or Mac Arthur, or Ted Kluszewski's prodigious home runs. It was a tranquil time, yet it was interlaced with a feverish need on the kids' part to pack every bit of action, every bit of fun into the hours between the end of supper and the moment when parents began ordering them inside for the night. Make no mistake about it, the evening meal was supper in College Hill. Clifton, Mount Airy, Western Hills, and other sections of the city might have referred to it as the dinner hour, but in our neighborhood it was supper. I'll bet even the Bartholomews called it supper. The setting sun clung fiercely to the sky, reluctant to let go of the day and the already considerable humidity caused arms and legs of participants of games to become slick and shiny. Everywhere, kids ran and laughed and screeched as shadows lengthened; and everywhere, the dogs ran and barked with them.

Summer nights also brought an element of danger to play on the street because you could not always see what was lurking behind garages, hedges and fences. Hide and seek, go sheepy go, and capture the leader were more fun at night because of the unknown. Even in familiar quarters, the games that required running up and down the block and in and out of alleys exposed one to attacks from unfriendly sources. A kid who harbored resentment from a daytime slight, perceived or real, could launch a rock or some other type of missile at an unsuspecting target from the cover of darkness. A group of kids might gang up on a "Snitch" or "Whiner" as they allegedly searched for the hider in the black recesses of unlit sheds or garages. Or, Spotty Morgan could spring from his front porch or a secluded place near his front yard, and chase you all the way home. Unlike our dog, Tippy, old Spotty gave no warning, no shrill bark, not even a growl. He just came at your ankles, full bore and malicious.

He also chased kids during the day, but then you usually saw him coming since everyone walked on the opposite side of the street from the Morgan house. If Grandpa was sitting on the front porch, it was foolish to tempt fate and walk or run or ride a bike immediately in front of their small, dark brick domicile, sheltered by mature oak trees, since he would undoubtedly set the malodorous canine on you, if the dog happened to be preoccupied with another task such as gnawing the head off a dead sparrow. Slowing to a walk, on the opposite side of the street, so as to keep a close watch on the Morgan residence became de rigueur for kids in our neighborhood. If a couple high school girls were sauntering along, you hurried or slowed to walk in proximity to them, assured that Grandpa had the field glasses trained on their legs, and was holding the beast at bay.

One day it did not work for me. I did not slow my normal trot quickly enough to allow Mary Ellen Harney to approach me when Spotty Morgan came tearing across the street ready to intercept my passage down the block to Billy Heinrich's house. If the dog was not acting unilaterally, then that old fox, Grandpa, figured he would release the hound to get me out of the picture, causing long legged Mary Ellen to temporarily freeze and give himself a longer than normal, slow motion viewing of one of the block's cuties. Whatever the reason, I made Jesse Owens look like he was standing still, as I shot past the snapping jaws of Spotty just as he reached my segment of sidewalk, past Billy's house, and around the far corner of my own home and into our side yard.

The dog had stopped chasing me as I had raced up and across our compact, slightly elevated front lawn. It was as if he knew I had left the public domain for private property, so it would be wise for him to cease and desist. As I came to an abrupt halt at our side door, I saw our neighbor, Mrs. Vaughn, watering the flowers along the side of her house. She smiled warmly at me and asked, "Was Spotty Morgan chasing you?"

Through gasps, and with a heaving chest, I affirmed that, indeed the vicious smelly little creature had chased me down the street, again.

Still smiling, she said, "I don't know what he'd do if he ever caught one of you kids. Probably tear a sneaker off and head home."

As I tried to think how a grown up would respond to this, she easily shifted gears and commented how hot that late afternoon was, and maybe everyone was using their garden hose at that precise time to wash cars, or squirt bathing suit clad youngsters, or attempt to water flowers as she was doing. The water barely trickled out of the hose onto her thirsty peonies and petunias, and this caused her to wonder if everyone was draining the city water supply in abundant amounts just then. "Look at that, " she said disgustedly, "I could spit better than that!"

Just like that, Spotty Morgan was forgotten. He was not important to her or to any of the adults in our world, but then, they did not have to skulk past his house every day, or risk having a bronzed ankle or calf chomped by the devilish mongrel. Being chased by, or outrunning, or out maneuvering Spotty was an exciting daily activity, to which we ascribed an element of danger or intrigue. It became common to ask any kid in the neighborhood that was breathless due to exertion or excitement if they had just outrun Spotty Morgan.

More than once, as I breathlessly entered our kitchen during those wondrous summers, screen door slamming behind me, I was told by my mother to calm down and compose myself before launching into the latest tale of neighborhood entanglement or machination. Then, before I could get a word out, she would say, "What's the matter, was Spotty Morgan chasing you?"

Spotty Morgan chased and terrorized kids all the time, and I cannot state exactly when it stopped being exciting or interesting for me, and instead simply became tiresome and a nuisance, but it happened. One evening at supper I told my dad I wished Spotty was dead. My father carefully studied my face and I felt uncomfortable. The rest of the family was silent as he explained that even though Spotty Morgan seemed terrible and vicious to me he was loved very much by his family, just as we loved Tippy. He explained that Spotty was growing older and one day Grandpa would not have him around to serve as his companion, and the kids on the street would probably miss seeing Spotty then also. He said I should not wish for anyone or anything to be dead or dying, as I would not want someone wishing harm on our family or dog.

I told my father that Tippy was different. He didn't just chase people needlessly. If he bit someone, or tore their pants, maybe they had it coming. I said no one, outside the Morgans loved Spotty, but all the neighbors liked Tippy.

One of my brothers snorted and said I should try telling that to anyone that Tippy had suddenly, and without warning, engaged in combat.

I said I did not care, and insisted the neighborhood would be better off without Spotty Morgan. My father sternly silenced me with, "You don't know what you're talking about. Now shut up and finish your supper. He's their dog, and he's important to them. You shouldn't be so mean."

In early summer the following year Spotty Morgan died. No one said how he died, whether it was old age or what, but he was suddenly gone from our world, gone from the lives of all the kids he had tormented. One late, hazy, humid July afternoon when a bunch of us were walking home after playing baseball in the park, we started talking about how quiet it seemed on the street, without Spotty chasing us. We were exactly opposite the Morgan residence, on the other side of the street where we always walked to avoid Spotty if we could, when Billy Heinrich stopped suddenly. Thumping a baseball steadily into his fielder's glove, he stared across the street at the Morgan house, and said Grandpa looked sad sitting on the porch all alone. He said he would bet that Grandpa felt lonely.

"How could you tell?" One of the boys said. "He never changes. He looks the same this year as he did last year. He probably don't even know Spotty's dead."

All of us laughed except Billy, who said, "I just know I'd miss my dog. I'd feel lonely."

I remembered Billy having said that three months later when Tippy became very sick, and could not climb out of his bed in our basement. It was a Saturday, and we could not get him to eat. By Sunday he was so sick even a drink of water caused him to vomit. He staggered when my mom or dad forced him to stand, so they could rearrange his bed and make him more comfortable. My brothers and I would pet him gently, and he would give us a small, painful wag of his tail, or he would try to lift his head in some manner of recognition, but his health deteriorated steadily. Veterinarians were not open on Sunday in those days, and people with suffering pets were expected to mercifully put them out of their misery in their own fashion. My mom would not allow my dad to take any such action, so he told her she would have to bundle Tippy into a small red wagon we had in the garage and take him to the vet's office on Monday morning. My father left for work two hours before the veterinarian's office was open, so it would be up to my mother to seek help for Tippy.

Monday morning was damp and cool, and we did not want to go to school knowing our dog, our companion, was sick down in the cellar. My father had gone to work, and we were finishing breakfast in the kitchen when we heard our mother's footsteps coming up from the basement. She tried hard to smile, but her lips quivered and her eyes began to tear. "Tippy's dead. He died this morning."

We began to cry and tell her we did not want to go to school. We couldn't go, not today!

She quieted us, and told us we **were** going to school, and that evening as soon as our father got home we would bury Tippy in the backyard, out behind the garage. She would call our dad at his store and tell him to come home as soon as he could, and maybe he could even close a little early if possible.

In the coming weeks I heard several soft conversations at the kitchen table among my father, my mother, and my uncle, long after the supper dishes had been washed and put away. I did my homework at that table, yet listened intently to what the adults were saying, as they drank a fresh pot of coffee, and the men smoked cigarettes. They had determined, based on how Tippy had died and what the veterinarian had told them after they described his condition and reactions that devastating weekend, that the dog had been poisoned. My dad thought someone in the neighborhood had fed something to him that made him sick enough to die a slow, painful death. My uncle agreed, and said there were probably several neighbors that had harbored hateful feelings about our pooch.

They talked and laughed of torn pants and neighborhood kids with sweaters and sweatshirts that had to be extracted from Tippy's teeth. Yes, there were people who probably were as glad to see Tippy gone as they were Spotty Morgan's departure. My father made this point quietly. I knew it was for my benefit, and I felt terribly sad and ashamed.

I could not stop thinking about Billy Heinrich's words. I felt lonely for weeks afterward, even after my father brought a new puppy home one evening. I finally told my father, one night right before I went to bed, that I was lonely without Tippy. I was glad we had the new dog, but I still missed Tippy. I told my dad I missed him as much as I was sure Grandpa missed Spotty Morgan. My father put his newspaper down, stubbed out his Chesterfield, and took me upstairs and tucked me into bed.